No One
Writes Back

TITLES IN THE LIBRARY OF KOREAN LITERATURE
AVAILABLE FROM DALKEY ARCHIVE PRESS

Library of Korean Literature
10

No One Writes Back

Jang Eun-jin

Translated by
Jung Yewon

DALKEY ARCHIVE PRESS
CHAMPAIGN / LONDON / DUBLIN

Originally published in Korean as *Amudo p'yŏnji haji ant'a* by Munhak Tongne, Paju, 2009

Library of Congress Cataloging-in-Publication Data

Jang, Eun-jin.
[Amudo p'yonji haji ant'a. English]
No one writes back / Jang Eun-jin ; translated by Jung Yewon. -- First edition.
pages cm
ISBN 978-1-56478-960-0 (acid-free paper)
1. Young men--Fiction. 2. Interpersonal communication--Fiction. 3. Letter writing--Fiction. I. Jung, Yewon, translator. II. Title.
PL994.14.U54A8213 2013
895.7'35--dc23
2013027139

Partially funded by a grant from the Illinois Arts Council, a state agency

Library of Korean Literature
Published in collaboration with the Literature Translation Institute of Korea

www.dalkeyarchive.com

Cover: design and composition by Mikhail Iliatov

I left home with an MP3 player and a novel in an old backpack. And with Wajo.

1. Motels are secretive.

And sometimes—no, often—no, almost always, they are suggestive.

According to a motel proprietor, most people use a motel as a "place of rest," or in other words, a place in which to have sex, and think of it as such. I used to think so too, though I've never been to a motel with a woman. But now, I had become, like them, a person who stops now and then to rest at a motel. The important thing is that I just rest. By "rest," I mean staying the night and taking a break. Sleeping, pure and simple.

When I walked into the Motel Iris with Wajo, however, my sleeping wasn't taken to be so pure and simple. So in order to get a room, we had to offer some words of explanation before offering money. Depending on who's listening, the words might come across as calm explanation, or mere excuses. The proprietor, a woman who was dozing off at the counter, looking disheveled despite the elegant name of the motel, automatically said when she saw us: "Are you here for a rest, or to stay the night?"

I had to choose one or the other. At such moments, it seemed as though an automated robot, programmed with the same words, stood at all motels nationwide. True, there isn't much of a choice when it comes to what to say to a customer who walks into a motel, no matter how hard you search a dictionary. Those two options suffice. The customers may even wish not to be asked those questions, because it's either embarrassing or bothersome.

It seemed that the proprietor wasn't fully awake when she asked the question; she looked from me to Wajo, frowning a little, with a knowing look in her eyes, a look that's usually intended for "couples." Perhaps all couples looked suggestive to motel proprietors. To us, however, "rest" just meant rest, and "sleep" just meant sleep, so choosing an option was meaningless. But having had plenty of experience with motels, we knew what kind of an answer would serve us better. We also knew that we had to choose an option.

So I said, with confidence, "We're staying the night."

What's odd is that the answer seemed to sound even more suggestive to the woman. She looked at us with even more suspicion. She seemed a little perplexed, too.

So in the end, I had to say—as a final offering of explanation before paying for the lodging—"It's a boy."

Wajo, being the smart boy he is, barked twice, "Woof, woof!" at the woman.

Then he lifted two legs into the air, startling her by revealing his big genitals. Finally, she gave us the key. We always have to work twice as hard as anyone to get a room.

2. Despite everything, the proprietor of Motel Iris is on the lenient side. Most people frown when I tell them that I'll be staying with a dog. They say things like, "We can't have our rooms smelling like dogs," "It's hard to clean dog hair off the bedding," "He's toilet trained, right?" "I'll have to ask the proprietor, because this has never happened before," and so on. Through experience, I've learned how to make them shut their mouths. I give them an extra ten thousand won bill. Usually, two people stay in one room in motels and inns, but even so, we have to pay an extra ten thousand won from time to time. To them, Wajo is a dog, and a dog is not a person but a thing, an additional thing which incurs additional cost. And they never turn down the offer of extra money. It's better, of course, than getting turned out.

Every time that happens, the people seem to be less than dogs in my eyes. Wajo is smarter than I am, and smarter than they are. He understands everything people say, so in many cases, he's even better than human. No, he's always better than human. And sometimes, he seems human. So I don't regret paying extra money on their demand. Lately, I've been giving them extra money before they even ask. I evaluate their character based on how they regard Wajo, and what they say about him. To the proprietor of Motel Iris, I gave an eighty. I took twenty points off because she suspected our relationship to be something abnormal.

3. As you've probably guessed, I'm a traveler who goes from motel to motel.

I had to give up or set aside many things to come on this journey: home, family, friends, a job, and love. In the first place, this journey wasn't meant as a means to gain something. I embarked upon the journey to rid myself of things, and it could only really begin when I did so. Still, there's probably a bit of something I hope to have gained by the end of the journey. If there is, it's probably something like quiet stability. It's a simple desire for me. To be honest, I think you should gain at least one thing from a long journey. If there was nothing to be gained, I'd feel wronged, and the people who have blabbed on about traveling in all those books, and urged others to travel, would feel ashamed. I'm not saying, however, that I began my journey after reading their books on travel.

I don't like travel books that are half full of photographs. Sometimes, you can't tell whether the book was written for travel, or the travel was undertaken for the book. What I dislike even more are people who like to show off their travels. You can't tell whether they travel for themselves, or to show other people. People who show off their travels do so because really, they don't have anything. That's why I don't take pictures when I travel. I don't buy souvenirs, either. Those things just get in the way when you travel. Travel means freedom.

I do, however, like to write when I travel. Written words are less extravagant than photographs and souvenirs, and they are serious and contemplative. Words penned while traveling do not lie; they're not for showing off, but for making you reflect on, and take care of, yourself. I dare say that in life, it is when we travel that our minds and hearts are the most open. It's a time when we think more than at any other time in our lives. We may even think of something that we would never have thought of in all our lives. And so, it would be the loss or the mistake of a lifetime not to write down in words those thoughts which may never have occurred to us. You can always go back and take pictures, and buy as many souvenirs as you want. But the thoughts that come to you while you travel will not come back. When you go back, the feelings and sensations you have will no longer be the ones you had before.

4. That's why I, when the day is over, settle down in a motel or an inn and write a letter before I do anything else. Washing up, eating, and resting come later. If I wash up or eat, I feel as though the day's worth of feelings goes down the drain and the esophagus altogether. The drain and the esophagus are places unknown to me. All I know is that they are dark, smelly, black, and long. I don't want to send my travels down to such places.

Letters, however, are all right. At least I know better than anyone the route through which letters travel. Better yet, if the address is correct, the route is neither dark nor smelly. So, because I must write a letter as soon as I arrive, the motels or inns where I stay are always places of letters for me. And for me, letters are daily necessities.

I take out from my backpack some sheets of paper and a pencil with an eraser on it, and lie down flat on the floor. I feel as though I've turned into an octopus. Wajo is lying down at the foot of the bed on the other side of the room, looking tired. Wajo can't write letters, but he is quite aware of me and my letter writing. The sound of the papers rustling, the sound of the pencil scratching the paper, the sound of the eraser at the tip of the pencil rubbing away at unsatisfactory sentences and wrong words—whenever sounds come flowing out of the letters, Wajo's wide and flat ears cock up. When they do, I wonder, is it possible that he understands what kind of sentences I'm writing? Wajo listens quietly to what I'm writing, and if he doesn't like it, he barks loudly, once. When I follow his advice and take another look at what I've written, sure enough, something is off or inappropriate. In this way, I reflect Wajo's opinions in my letters. This journey is for both Wajo and me, and since it can be termed, if necessary, a "journey of letters," I think he has the right to take part in the letter writing.

I mull over the appropriate recipient of the letter containing today's journey. The faces of people with a number on the left side of their chest go round and round in my head. Someone who would best fit the kind of journey we had today; someone who would understand our story better than anyone else; and someone who would thus keep the letter safe without throwing it away. 239.

5. 239 was a high school girl I met at a bus stop while waiting for a bus headed for an unknown city. 239 is the number with which

I designated the girl. Saying that, I feel like one of those machines on bank windows that spit out number slips, but I keep a tab on the people I meet on my journey with numbers. Numbers are the simplest way to establish an order, and are easy to remember, too. Above all, numbers are signs that are infinitely expandable, with no risk of depletion, which is an attractive idea.

Numbers are a means through which I identify people. Simple as they look, numbers contain a myriad of information. They are like product barcodes. I touch Number 239 with an imaginary barcode reader. With a beep, information on 239 pours out onto the virtual monitor in my mind. I focus on the information listed on the monitor.

Two best friends. No boyfriend. Has a black cat. Average grades. Loathes her math teacher more than anyone after her father. Wants to study drama and film. Unfortunately, does not have a face fit for an actress. Still, wants to be an understudy, at least. Porn actress a possibility. Her father keeps beating her. Her mother has been having an affair for two years with the plastic surgeon who gave her a chin job. Only 239 knows this fact. Is begging her mother for double eyelid surgery. If her mother refuses, she will expose the affair to her father. Worships the Beatles and Robert De Niro. Does not read books of poetry, because they don't have an ending. Thinks there has to be an ending for despair to end as well. Has considered suicide.

6. As is the case with everyone at that age, 239 was anguishing between youth and despair. Because youth is so beautiful in itself, I felt as though I had tasted the most extreme despair when the word "despair" came popping out of 239's mouth. I thought back to myself when I was 239's age. At the time, my despair was over one thing only—my stuttering. I learned at that age, however, that the one despair brought with it a noisy cart full of countless despairs.

Never had more than two best friends, due to a stuttering problem. Hated my Korean teacher, who often called on me to read aloud in class, to the point of wanting to kill her. So, out of pride, often declared that my dream was to be an announcer. Because of that, my family and other kids looked at me with pity in their eyes. Thought in the end that I'd be satisfied with being a voice actor specializing in moaning. Was beaten time and time again by my older brother who was ashamed of his stuttering brother. My father blamed my mother, saying that I was born that way because she was too devoted to her job as a math teacher and worked like crazy on calculus problems during her pregnancy. My mother countered that I took after him, who studied physics in college, which led to frequent fights. Naturally led to say less and less, stayed cooped up in a little room with a poster of Olivia Hussey on the wall, and read aloud from nothing but novels. The novels had to be thick. They had to be thick so that I could go on practicing speaking without stopping. Thought from time to time about biting my own tongue and dying.

7. A youth in despair, and a youth who was once in despair, seem to have something in common. There may not be as many kinds of despair facing humankind as we think. As in, "Are you here to rest, or to stay the night?" We can't, of course, choose the kind of despair we are to face, in the same way as we choose between the two options at a motel counter. The good thing, though, is that there's only one way to overcome despair. So we don't have go through the painful process of choosing. That one way is to grit your teeth and go on living without dying.

I write a letter to 239, pressing down hard with the pencil. The letter starts out by talking about 750, whom I met today. Lead powder spreads out on the paper. Little by little, the lead grows duller, and as it does, the sentences come into being.

750 was someone I met on the playground of an elementary school that had closed down. There was no one else on the playground. 750 was sitting atop the highest pull-up bar, swaying his legs, and staring intently off somewhere. In his hand was a palm-sized book. Hanging from a lower pull-up bar next to him, I asked him what he was looking at.

"The 5-3 classroom," he said in reply.

"Is that where you studied?"

"It's where I studied, and where I pushed a friend from the window."

"Huh? How . . . Is he dead, by chance?"

"He might as well be."

"What do you mean, he might as well be?"

"He's been in a coma. For twenty years."

"What did your friend do to you?"

"He hid my shoes."

"And you couldn't go home?"

"I stayed up the night in the classroom. My feet were very cold, because it was winter."

"No wonder you were angry at your friend."

"He must be angrier at me now, though. So I've been reading him poems at his bedside, asking for forgiveness."

"For twenty years?"

"Yes. It was his dream to become a poet."

"You must have read him a lot of poems."

"I feel like I know all the poems in the world. But it looks like tomorrow will be the last day."

"Are you going somewhere?"

"My friend is . . . They've decided today to disconnect the respirator."

"The pain will be over, at least."

"I buried my first cat a few days ago, in the spot where my friend fell."

"How did it die?"

"The vet recommended euthanasia."

"Does that mean that your poems will come to an end, too?"

"No. I'm going to sit here and read poems for my friend and my cat."

"Until when?"

"Until he's buried underground."

750 opened his book of poems. It seemed that 750's despair would have no ending, like books of poetry. The good thing, though, is that poems and poets will continue to be born, and the poems that are to be read by 750, like numbers, will never be depleted. At that moment, the book of poems looked like an object that held the essence of life.

8. I write letters because I want to convey to someone the stories of these people, but also because I want to let someone know that a day had existed for me as well. Letters, in other words, are like journal entries to me. The only difference is that the day does not stay with me, but is sent to someone else. Journals are monopolized, but letters are shared. Journals are kept by one person alone, but letters are kept by two or more people. I began to obsess over letters when I became acutely aware of the notion of "two." While traveling, you grow even more aware of the notion. Perhaps that's why I began my journey.

I ask at the end of the letter to send a reply within two days, adding, "From Room 203 at Motel Iris," and seal the envelope. My day vanishes into the envelope. All the letters in the world have a look of importance to them, and now, the day, confined in a rectangular frame, finally takes on the same important look.

I write down 239's address and my own on the envelope. I put down 239 as the name of the recipient. Receiving the letter, 239 will be reminded of the code number I gave her. She'll also remember suddenly, like a dream she'd had the night before, the words I said: "You're the 239th person I've met. Don't forget your number, 239." Finally, I stick a stamp firmly on the envelope so it won't slip off. A day may come when I write of 239 to 750.

Thus ends my weary day. My days start and end with letters. Since I'm done with my letter writing, it is now 0 o'clock, when another day begins for me. Maybe I'm someone who ends yesterdays and begins tomorrows earlier than others. So I may grow old and get wrinkles sooner than others. If any changes come because I get wrinkles sooner than others, they would probably consist of quick resignation and an awareness of reality. So getting wrinkles isn't such a bad thing.

After I seal up the envelope, my body begins to relax, and I grow drowsy. I never feel drowsy before I'm finished with my letter writing, no matter how tired I am. But I need to eat before I sleep. It doesn't matter if I skip a meal, but I can't let Wajo starve. Not starving Wajo was my grandfather's greatest aim in life when he was alive. It was also the last will he dictated.

9. I think I should go to a convenience store nearby and get something to eat. Wajo's food is nearly gone, too. It's nowhere near enough to fill his stomach.

I get up, and am about to put my shoes on, when Wajo bolts upright and begins to sniff and perk up his ears. He won't understand that I'm trying to be considerate by sneaking off on my own. His ears and nose have become three or four times as keen as before. He doesn't know what it means for people to be considerate of him. He only knows that he has to be considerate of people. It can't be helped, for he has been trained to be mindful of human beings. I have no choice but to take him with me.

I wonder how much more time must pass before he forgets his nature. Unlike humans, dogs don't seem to know what it is to forget. If a dog has been trained not to forget, shouldn't it be trained again to forget what it has learned before, when the knowledge becomes useless? The life of a dog is a life, too, and changes are bound to occur in life, so shouldn't readjustments be made to fit the changes?

I put the leash around Wajo's neck and step out of the motel.

10. The convenience store sign shines brightly. Sometimes, I think that these signs emit the brightest lights in the city. Whenever I go past the light into a convenience store, I think of 56. 56 is someone I met while eating cup noodles at a convenience store table.

I was breaking my wooden chopsticks in half when 56 said to me, "When is a convenience store most like a convenience store?"

Because of his question, the chopsticks didn't break evenly. I grow a little nervous whenever I break wooden chopsticks, because if they don't break evenly, I can't maneuver them evenly.

Frowning, I said, "I guess when I feel convenienced, since it's a convenience store."

56 sat up straighter, with a look on his face that said he hadn't expected me to answer his question. But for me, such a reaction was even more unexpected. I was a traveler, and traveling is an action taken to make it easier for strangers to approach you, and it becomes meaningful only when you approach strangers with ease. If you think about it, the purpose of travel isn't to see the scenery or architecture. The scenery and architecture are important, too,

but I always thought that they came after people. 56 began to share with me his ideas on "when a convenience store is most like a convenience store," saying that I was the only person who had ever answered his question.

"You're wrong. It's when you're eating cup noodles. Without cup noodles, a convenience store is nothing but a corpse. Isn't it fantastic? You just pay for the noodles, and they give you hot water for free, and a seat, and even let you throw away the trash after you've eaten. I can't understand people who eat cup noodles at home. That's something that defies cup noodles' reason for existence," he said.

"So cup noodles are the symbol of convenience stores?" I asked.

"That's a great way to put it. Sometimes I wish that they sold only cup noodles at convenience stores."

"Do you eat cup noodles often?"

"Almost every day. Above all, they're cheap, easy to prepare, and taste good, too."

"And there's a great variety of them."

"Right. When they give you options, it means they don't look down on you."

"You've never had them at home?"

56 didn't answer. We talked about cup noodles until we had emptied our cups. I found out then that there's a lot to be said about cup noodles alone.

After polishing off the last drop of the soup, I asked him suddenly, "Can I write you a letter later?"

"A letter? Sure. That sounds hot somehow, like cup noodles," he said.

"What's your address?"

"My e-mail address is . . ."

"No, I mean your home address."

56 clammed up again. Finally, I understood. 56 had no address.

As long as he didn't have an address, a convenience store would always be most like a convenience store. One of the rules I had set down on this journey was to give a number to only those who gave me their address. Nonetheless, I gave him a number—56. For 56, I just wanted to do it, regardless of the rules. So 56 was the only one who had a number without an address. And the only one who couldn't receive my letter. Even now, 56 is probably going from one convenience store to another, somewhere in this cold city, eating hot cup noodles.

I'm about to pick up some *samgak gimbap*, but change my mind and head toward the cup noodle shelf, thinking I should eat the symbol of convenience stores since I was at one. Just as 56 said, there's a great variety, and I don't feel looked down upon. But seeing as how I want to try the shrimp flavor as well as the kimchi flavor, and even the black bean flavor as I walk down the aisle, I wonder if the variety isn't there just to incite your desire, pretending not to look down on you. After all, even someone without an address needs desire. It seems, however, that humans can't free themselves of choices and decisions, no matter where they go. Life doesn't go on if you don't choose one thing or another.

After racking my brain, I finally decide on the shrimp flavor, and buy some fishcakes and ham for Wajo, as well. Since I met 56, I never have cup noodles in a room at a motel or an inn. Cup noodles seem to taste best when I eat them at a convenience store. The soup warms my insides. The soup must be too hot. It makes me want to tell someone in a letter that they should try some cup noodles at a convenience store, if they want to feel that a convenience store is indeed most like a convenience store.

11. After finishing my meal, I come back to the motel with a beer and some nachos. The proprietor at the counter still looks at us

with suspicion in her eyes. I take ten points off her character.

I put the beer and the nachos down on the bed, and go into the bathroom to take a shower. I wash my hair, and then my underwear, and hang it to dry. I threw away a pair of underwear with holes in it, so I have to stay naked until the underwear dries. The greatest burden for a traveler is his clothes. Two pairs of underwear and one outer layer of clothing will suffice. I buy new clothes only when my old ones gets tattered or so torn I can no longer wear them. People who care about appearances can never travel. In some cases, of course, circumstances naturally prevent you from caring about appearances.

My younger sister is a case in point of someone who can't travel because of her clothes or appearance. She has never traveled, for she dreads getting ready for a trip. She has tried, of course, several times to go on a trip. The problem was that as she packed this and that, her luggage increased, and in the end, she couldn't go anywhere because of too much luggage.

I say from time to time, if you want to know about someone else's desires, you should have them pack a suitcase. Or take a peek into their suitcase. Someone who packs his bag with all kinds of stuff ends up suffering from just that much fatigue and stress, even while traveling. The weight of the bag alone will guarantee that. The trip, intended as a way to unburden yourself, suddenly becomes a burden in itself. People who care about what other people think of them, like my sister, can never go on a trip.

Instead, my sister planned other trips—trips to the department store, on which she wore high heels and carried a purse. She insists to whoever's next to her that shopping is a form of traveling, too. It's a good thing that at least she doesn't say she's back from traveling when she's back from shopping.

"All you do is g-go spend money—th-that's not traveling," I said.

"Your feet hurt, and you get something out of it, so it's the same thing. Do you know what an incredible thing it is to walk around in high heels? It's a lot more ascetic than the travels you talk about," she said.

My sister always sounded nervous, sharp, and edgy, like someone with a mental disorder.

"W-why would you t-take it upon yourself to do something like that?" I asked.

"Because at least it's less painful than when people stare at me like I'm an ugly monkey," she replied.

" . . . "

Whenever my sister came back from her trips to the department store, both her arms would be laden with shopping bags like clusters of apples. She looked even more tired coming back from her trips. She didn't gain any wisdom, even as she picked and ate the apples that hung from her arms. The apples only enticed—when she bit into them, they didn't taste like anything at all. Nevertheless, my sister's journeys for sweet apples that did not exist never came to an end. She spent nearly all her income adorning herself. The only thing that can stop the rule of desire is death. My sister won't be able to change her habits until the day she dies.

12. I have a beer, sitting naked on the bed. Now and then, the sound of a girl's lilting laughter and moans float over from the room next door. I am startled, having forgotten that some people really do opt for "a rest." Because of them, motels once again become secretive, very suggestive places. I look down at my naked body. I laugh, thinking that the lovers next door and I probably don't look all that different. Nude is the most appropriate attire for a motel.

There's one question that comes to my mind whenever such sounds of excitement reach my ears. Are they doing it with the lights on, or off? There was a way I could check, by going outside and looking up at the windows, but I can't go out in this state. If someone asked, I'd say that I would do it with the lights on. When I turn the lights off, I imagine all places to be like my home, and then I can't do anything. I wouldn't be able to feel a girl's breasts, let alone get an erection, and she would turn her cold back on me.

When I left home, I suffered from a phobia. At first, I thought I'd come down with claustrophobia, like the peculiar Mr. Sommer in Patrick Suskind's *The Story of Mr. Sommer*. I found out by chance that it wasn't claustrophobia, but phobia of a certain place, when I went over to my friend's house. Surprisingly, there wasn't the slightest sign of my seizures, which had continued on for some time, even though his house was small, filthy as a dumping ground, and smelly—the kind of a place that would make even normal people go into a seizure. Thinking it odd, I stayed at another friend's the next day, and at another friend's after that for a few days. Still, my seizures didn't return, and I went back home, thinking I was better now. But as soon I stepped in through the door, the awful seizures started again. I had cold sweat running down my back, I felt nervous, I couldn't digest food, and I couldn't sleep. I ran away again to my friend's, feeling as though I would die at any moment. A writer once said that home could heal your sicknesses and bring you happiness, but in my case, the opposite was true.

That's how I came to quit my job, and decided to come on this journey. I could sleep comfortably anywhere, as long as the place didn't look like my house. Luckily, the house wasn't one of those apartments which were exact replicas of each other. So for me, the place of safety wasn't my house, measuring 45 *pyeong*, but the entire earth except for those 45 *pyeong*. To put it another way, I had lost the desire to possess a place of my own, with decent furniture.

13. Instead, a desire for words swelled up in me around that time. It was my friend who lived in the filthy, smelly house who first sensed my desire.

The night I stayed over at his house, he said to me, "You seem smarter in some way."

"What do you mean?" I asked.

"That's it, exactly."

"Wh-what do you mean by 'that?'"

"That. Before, you would have said, 'Wh-wh-what do you mean by that?' but now, you're saying, 'Wh-what do you mean by that?'"

Suddenly, it dawned on me that I was beginning to talk again. I told my friend to keep talking to me, and he really kept talking to me all night. Later on, he even asked some weird questions, such as, "Have you slept with Yuseon?" and "How many girls have you slept with so far?" My words sounded smarter, less stunted, even to myself. Now that I sounded smart, I didn't feel like an idiot when I said I'd slept with only three girls, at my age.

In the end, I got so ambitious that I came to wish that I could talk without stuttering at all. I wanted to use this chance to fix my problem, once and for all. It seemed, too, that since I would be able to survive only if I talked well and often, I shouldn't neglect the problem any longer. Words equaled communication, and I, more than anyone else, was someone who could survive only through communication.

I never used to initiate conversations, and I couldn't even answer questions very well, but the next night, I kept talking to my friend.

"Have you ever slept with S-Sugyeong?" I asked, and went on to ask, "How m-many times have you s-slept with girls?"

He said he'd slept with Sugyeong the night they started going out, and said he'd slept about a hundred times with girls, adding that only an idiot would keep count of each and every time he slept with a girl. Because his words were smart, he sounded manly, and seemed like an incredible person. He even looked decent and honorable. I wanted to go on talking because I wanted to look as cool as he did, and I felt confident that I could; I even felt that I could make the arduous effort required to change "Wh-what do you mean?" to "What do you mean?"

Exhausted from keeping the conversation going with my friend, I fell into deep thought that night before sleep. What if I went from place to place, talking to people, since I couldn't go home anyway because of my seizures? My journey, thus begun, has continued for nearly three years. And I no longer stutter. Not only that, I've learned how to approach strangers and initiate conversations. For instance, I'd say, "Excuse me, Miss, you have a run in your stocking." The problem is that occasionally, I can't tell between the things I should and shouldn't say.

14. So this journey is a means by which I can survive without dying, a measure by which I can grow stronger through words, and an experiment through which I can confront the world. If no one listened to and understood my words and thoughts, they would be meaningless. That's why I had to meet someone, anyone, and talk to them. To do that, I had to walk; I had to go somewhere, anywhere. If I got tired of the street, my obsession might get tired of me and leave me too, I thought.

I think I've grown somewhat, for sure, during the three years I've traveled. That's what it means to be alone, to look after yourself. My growth, which had come to a stop three years ago, seems to have come to a completion now, at last. I no longer seek change by running after it. That doesn't mean, however, that I want to walk ahead of, or next to, change. If I can detect change, that's quite enough.

15. After finishing the beer, I close my eyes, leaving the lights on. I can hear the sound of Wajo snoring now and then, and the sound of the lovers next door opening the door and leaving. I feel like listening to the Beatles. I take out my MP3 player with its 2,300 songs from my backpack, and put on the earphones.

16. The underwear is completely dry. The good thing about summer is that laundry dries fast. Even if it's not dry, you can put it on and it doesn't matter, in summer. Winter isn't an appropriate season for drying jeans or traveling. Before I leave the room, I squeeze myself in under the bathroom sink, and write a short sentence with a marker on the underside of the sink: August 3, 2009. Wajo and I were here.

The reason why I leave a mark on the underside of the sink, of all places, is because out of all the things comprising a motel, that's the spot that's the hardest to see. The harder it is to see, the lower the likelihood of it being discovered and removed. Because of the low likelihood of it being discovered, the person who discovers it becomes seized with a sense of wonder. And above all, there's something secretive about words that can be found only when you cram your head in with difficulty.

I take the room key to the counter. The feeling of emptiness that comes over me every time I leave a room returns as usual, never to be gotten rid of, like a tattoo. It's because I sense that I'll never be able to return to this place. It would be nice if the person I wrote to in this room happened to stay here, some distant day in the future. When she does, the sentence on the sink will be a secret between 239 and me, as furtive as a motel. I think at least one secret should be shared between those who write each other letters. If a journal entry is a one-man crime, a letter is a joint principal offender, or an abettor.

Taking the key from me, the proprietor looks at Wajo and

says he's handsome, and asks how old he is. Like everyone who has a dog, I like it very much when people show interest in Wajo. I feel offended for no reason when they don't. Since she did show interest, her character, which had lost some points, gains some back. Wajo is thirteen years old. He's an old man in human years.

"He's the same kind of dog that's in the movie, *Maeumi*, right?" she asks.

"Yeah, a Labrador retriever."

"What's his name?"

"Wajo."

"That dog was a good actor, too."

What does she mean by "too?" Has she figured it out already?

As though in acknowledging a fact, I say, "He's a pretty good actor himself."

She gives Wajo a piece of leftover bread.

Wajo lifts one leg upon leaving Motel Iris, peeing on the door. It's his private ritual. Like the sentence I left on the sink.

17. After leaving the motel, I look for the nearest mailbox. It's quite difficult to find a mailbox these days. After walking two hundred meters, I finally see a clumsy looking mailbox standing blankly next to the police station.

I stand before the mailbox, fidgeting with the letter for a long time. It's not that I want to open it. I never open an envelope I've sealed. Reading over a letter you wrote the night before is an act of denying yourself. When you read it over, you're bound to find at least one or two sentences you want to erase, like a mistake you made in the past. I don't think you need to be ashamed of them, since they're symptoms that occurred because you were too true to your feelings, or because you were full of courage. If we don't allow ourselves to have courage at night, at least, we'll have to live as cowards all our lives. I push the letter into the slot. The letter drops, with a light thud, to the bottom of the empty mailbox. I've grown accustomed to the sound.

The first thing I do after mailing a letter is find a phone booth. Finding a pay phone is even more difficult than finding a mailbox. I walk about four hundred more meters from the mailbox before I finally spot a phone booth. I deposit coins and call my friend. It's the friend who lives in a filthy, smelly house. After about twenty rings, I finally hear the sound of the coins drop. The sun is high in the sky, but my friend's voice comes out from the middle of the night.

"I'm your wake-up call now, huh?" I say.

"It doesn't really wake me up, though," he says.

"It's been three years, so you're too used to it. No wonder it doesn't wake you up."

"It's because you sound smart now. When you stuttered, I felt so frustrated that I just woke up."

"Should I pretend to stutter?"

"I'd rather hear you groan."

My friend lets out a long yawn. I wait politely for the yawn to end, and ask, "Any letters?"

I tense up.

"No," he says.

The answer is simple and clear as usual. The tension subsides, and a sense of frustration takes its place.

"Don't you find it a little inconvenient?"

"You find me inconvenient?"

"I like getting morning calls from you, but if you had a cell phone, I could call you or text you right away. If I do, that'd be the signal."

"If that were the case, you and I wouldn't have talked once on the phone."

"Well, that's true . . ."

"And if I took it as a signal when you were just calling to say hi, I'd be really disappointed later on."

"True . . ."

This friend who lives in a filthy, smelly house lives so close to my house that we're practically next door neighbors. I call him every other day to ask him if any letters have come for me, and if they have, to ask him to keep them safe so that they won't get into anyone else's hands or get wet in the rain. Luckily, he's out of a job so he has plenty of time on his hands. He must have felt bad for me, because for the first half year, he was faithful in granting my request. He dropped by my house every morning and afternoon to see if there were any letters.

During that half year, however, not a single letter came for me. He must have grown a little tired of coming and going, for he told me that he'd gotten a high-tech telescope. He said that with the telescope, he could see from his apartment whether any letters had been delivered, without going himself. Later he boasted that thanks to me, he'd found a fascinating hobby using the telescope. He seemed completely absorbed in sneaking peeks into apartments in which girls lived alone. He even told me that he had found someone totally hot, and said we should watch her together when I returned.

I knew why he'd gotten the telescope. He must have decided that using a telescope was much more practical than wasting his energy, taking the elevator down and then up again, for letters that never came. The telescope was something useful that kept him from making the trips in vain. And now that he had a telescope, I didn't feel as bad. My request was no longer a burden to him, and I even wished I had suggested it myself.

"It's about time you gave up. Not a single letter has come so far—do you think they'll suddenly start coming?" he says.

In spite of such words, he hasn't given up, either, because

every time I call, he tells me whether or not any letters have come. Maybe he longs for letters even more than I do, as though they were supposed to be for him. Of course, enough time had passed for him to start thinking that maybe they were for him, indeed.

"Things always happen suddenly," I say, and hang up after telling him I'll call again.

18. No one wrote today.

19. I stand for a long time in front of the mailbox, not knowing where to go, like a lost child. My mind goes blank. I come to myself at the sound of Wajo barking. I look around me. Which way should I go? My fate depends on the direction I take. I don't think I can come to an easy decision today. At times like this, it's best to leave it to Wajo. His instinct in choosing a direction is so brilliant that it's never disappointed me. At my request, Wajo lifts his head slightly, sniffs, and turns a circle. He's smelling the wind. Then he decides on a direction, and starts to walk. I follow blindly, with his leash tugging me. At times like this, I feel like Wajo is human, and I'm a dog.

Wajo comes to a stop at the subway station. Subways are somewhat difficult to get on with a dog. Sometimes, entrance is banned; often, people kick Wajo, saying there isn't enough space for people as it is. It isn't impossible, though. I think I'm going to resort to what I often do.

20. I go down the stairs and into the restroom in the subway station. I take a piece of yellow fluorescent clothing out of my backpack, and a pair of dark sunglasses from the case. The preparation is simple. All we have to do now is show off great acting skills as a team.

I fix my glance straight ahead, and hold tight onto Wajo's leash as though it were my lifeline. All eyes turn at once to the words, "Guide Dog," on Wajo's fluorescent clothing. There's quite a difference in the way people see Wajo, when he's wearing his guide dog outfit, and when he's just an ordinary dog. Wearing the outfit, Wajo turns into a laudable, marvelous, dignified dog. He becomes a good, meek, clean dog that would never bite or harm humans. On the other hand, Wajo, the ordinary dog, becomes a common mongrel that isn't even toilet trained. It's the same with me. All I do is put on a pair of sunglasses, and suddenly, people look at me with pity in their eyes, saying, "Oh, the poor man." It's only natural. They look at the disabled in a different light, because in their minds, people with disabilities are different from themselves. They look at the disabled in one of two ways: with pity or exclusion. Despite everything, pity is slightly better than exclusion.

Because of the way people regard us, we pass through the turnstile, the first hurdle, with no restrictions. The act is for Wajo, not for me. We do this not to deceive others, but to protect ourselves.

We hear the subway train approaching. We move toward the safety line. When I pull the leash downward, ever so slightly, Wajo places his rear end precisely and safely outside the yellow safety line. I stop right beside him. People send a round of applause to Wajo, who has accomplished his first mission with great success.

The subway train comes to a stop. The doors open, and people, looking exhausted, get off like loads of baggage. People using the same door we're using don't step in before Wajo. When people encounter the disabled, the first thing they do is shrink back. What they're showing me now is either subconscious courtesy or pity. It's either consideration or concession. With the courtesy and pity, and consideration and concession extended toward me, I make my way into the subway. A young man who has been shaking his head to the music on his MP3 player springs to his feet, as he has been taught, and yields his seat. It's possible that he's trying to avoid us. People don't yield their seats only because I'm a social minority. Yielding their seats, for them, isn't a difficult thing. By doing so, they confirm their normality, and feel relieved. I must sit down, so that they may feel relieved. As though I really were blind. As though that were the only role for the disabled to play. If not, they'd feel anxious and uncomfortable.

I observe those who are normal through the eyes of a blind man. I take a peek at their actions and into their hearts, through the dark sunglasses. It's fascinating to confirm the truth about other people through fake acts. The easiest way to confirm the truth is to put it through the litmus test of deceit. That's why people are interested in lies, tell them often, and go wild over them. That's why lies must exist.

21. Both Wajo and I are dozing off. Neither of us has to get off at any station, so we don't even pay attention to the announcements. It feels like a lot of time has passed. Then I hear a roaring voice. I turn my head toward the voice. But I'm a blind man, and must not look openly. I turn my head slightly, and observe the situation through the movement of my pupils only.

A woman is standing in the middle of the subway compartment. Like me, she's carrying a backpack, and next to her is a small handcart with wheels. A plastic bin is tied to the top of the cart, which fits perfectly. She takes something out of the bin and begins to talk to the passengers.

"Hi, I'd like to tell you about a book," she says.

She's trying to sell books on the subway. True, the subway is a good place in which to sell things. All kinds of things are sold on the subway, since all kinds of people use it. Things sold on the subway include air freshener, shoe polish, drain cleaners, fan covers, umbrellas, and even globes. So there's no reason why books shouldn't be sold. In fact, books seem even more appropriate than fan covers and umbrellas. People might complain if you open an umbrella on the subway, where there's no chance of rain, but you can open a book without worrying about what people might think. Besides, people have been saying lately that you should read books, at least on the subway. Still, it's a very strange scene. You can pick out any umbrella, and it would be as good as any other umbrella; books, however, can't be bought at random. It seems that the woman has only one title. In a day and age when life goes on only when you make choices and decisions, she seems like someone who has come to deprive you of the right to choose and decide. In a way, she's forcing you.

22. She says what she has to say and places one book on each passenger's lap, the way all vendors do. She puts one on mine, too. Do I look normal to her? Or is it a way of expressing a progressive statement that equal rights should be given to the handicapped, too, that they shouldn't be discriminated against?

She returns to the cart, and lifting a book says to the passengers, "If you say the right thing, I'll give you a discount."

Then she takes out a harmonica from her pocket, and begins to play. She's extremely good. She seems to be saying that we should take a look at the product until the music ends. Pretending to fumble with the book, I take a look, my eyes cast down. *Toothpaste and Soap*, the title reads. I open the book, and quickly take in the first sentence: "Today, I ate toothpaste. Tomorrow, I will eat soap."

The book is a full-length novel. I want to buy it, because the title and the first sentence fascinate me. But I'm a blind man at the moment, and shouldn't find it fascinating. I know nothing, for I see nothing. So I can't buy it. Even the normal people, however, who know everything, don't buy the book. Most passengers don't even pay any attention to the book, and focus only on their own thoughts. The books are returned to the woman.

If they had been umbrellas, she might have sold at least one. The normal people might have thought that the normal thing to do is to buy books at a bookstore. They might have felt suspicious because she didn't seem like a famous writer, or they might have felt offended because they felt as though they were being forced to buy the book. Or maybe they thought it was too expensive compared to other things sold on the subway, which usually cost about one or two thousand won, and didn't reach for their wallet for that reason. They might have been interested if it had been a book like *Making a Hundred Million Won a Month*, and not a novel. Maybe the woman's intention wasn't to sell the book—maybe she was doing her job as a part of a new marketing strategy designed by a publishing company. If it was indeed a strategy, then at least it informed a few people that a book called *Toothpaste and Soap* exists in the world.

23. The woman puts the books into the plastic bin, pulls the cart over to a seat across from me, and sits down. We're sitting face to face. She looks dejected, not having sold a single copy. I wonder, why does she sell books on the subway? And why just one title? And why, of all things, a novel? She stares intently at me, as if she has read my mind. She seems to be looking at me, aware that I'm blind. Then she grins, her teeth showing through. She seems to be grinning at me, aware that I'm not blind. I can't be found out here, so I, too, stare intently at her without budging an inch, pretending that I'm not aware of her.

Right then, she takes something out of her backpack. It's a

digital camera. She isn't taking a picture of me, is she? I wonder. But she is. She takes a picture of me with the camera. I'm supposed to be blind, so I can't stop her. Just then, the announcement comes on. I think I should get off.

I take Wajo's leash, get up with wavering steps, and walk toward the door as though my destination has finally been announced. I see the woman's reflection on the window. She's still staring at me. And she grins once more. It's starting to get creepy. I wish the subway would come to a stop soon. Why does the number 751 suddenly come to my mind at this moment? Why do I get the ominous feeling that I'll be designating her with the number? The subway comes to a stop. I get off the subway with quick, nimble steps, not like those of a blind man.

24. Ominous feelings are always right. The woman, pulling her cart, follows as if to tail us. It's as if she knows me. Could she be someone I went to elementary school with? Or could it be that she's someone I know but haven't recognized? It's true that I've met all kinds of people while traveling for three years. There were bad people, of course, but there were a lot more good people. People tend to remember bad things before the good, and more vividly and for a longer period of time, too. She's still a good person, compared to the person who pulled a knife on me, who remains a vivid bad memory. I might have been mistaken; maybe we're just going in the same direction, so I suddenly head toward a nearby takeout coffee shop. It's around dinnertime, so I'm feeling hungry, too. You're always hungry when you're on the road, even if you've just eaten. I order three sandwiches and a Coke. Will she pass me by, or not? I feel anxious as time goes by.

"Here's your order. It's eighty-six hundred won," the staff says.

I reach for my back pocket to get some money out. But my

wallet's gone. I look to the right. I don't see the woman. I feel relieved. But whatever happened to my wallet? Where could I have dropped it? I turn my head the other way. The woman is standing next to me, like a ghost. I forget my role as a blind man, and yelp. Not because she's standing like a ghost, but because she's holding my wallet. Did she pick my pocket? She's not decent; how could she steal a blind man's wallet? She moves her hand holding the wallet twice, distinctly, gesturing for me to take it. The gesture is possible only because she knows that I'm not blind. Did she give me that book on the subway for the same reason?

The staff looks at me, as though to urge me on. Since I have to pay before I do anything else, I take my wallet from her at once. I open it with ease, for I'm not blind. But the wallet is empty. No bills, no cash card, not even a coin. I glare at the woman through my sunglasses. She isn't a decent person after all. Then she makes an additional order of a sandwich and an ice coffee, and pays for both orders with money from her own wallet. Is she decent?

25. "Wh-who are you?"

In critical situations, I relapse into my stutter without even realizing it. The woman pushes the sandwiches and Coke toward me, as if doing me a generous favor. I feel a little ashamed, but I take them after some hesitation, since my wallet is empty and I'd have to starve if I missed this opportunity. When you travel, you often have to debase yourself. She cuts two of the sandwiches in half and puts them on a sheet of newspaper for Wajo, so that he'd have an easier time eating it. Wajo waits for me to give him the go-ahead. I hesitate, and then tell him to go ahead and eat. He devours them in haste, without a thought as to how I feel.

"I saw a pickpocket stealing your wallet," the woman says.

"On the subway?"

"When you were going through the turnstile."

33

"That's when you began watching me?"

"I began watching you long before that."

"When?"

"When you put the letter in the mailbox."

So she knew everything. I begin to stutter again.

"H-how come you had the wallet th-that the pickpocket stole?"

"He took out the cash and the cards, and threw it in the trash, so I got it out of there."

"You're not the pickpocket?"

"I don't think you're in a position to suspect me. Why don't you take those sunglasses off?"

She takes another bite of her sandwich. I, too, take a bite of my sandwich, with nothing more to say.

"So, you followed me to give me my wallet?"

"I thought you wouldn't have any money for food."

You have to be careful when people are kind to you for no reason.

I ask, with more caution in my voice, "Why did you follow me before that?"

"It surprised me that someone was putting a letter in a mailbox. What surprised me even more, though, was that you were pretending to be blind. Why? I'm curious," she said, her daring eyes glowing like light bulbs.

"You must be one of those people who can't stand not to know the answer to a question," I say.

"That's right, though I can stand hunger."

"Did you buy me the sandwich because you wanted to know my reason? So this is the price?"

"I see that the sandwich is half gone already. And that dog has licked everything up," she says.

"Why do you keep talking down to me?"

"It's a quick way to make friends. Don't you know that a river lies between the honorific and the common forms of speech?"

"I don't want to be friends with you."

"There's nothing for you to lose."

"Why do you want to be friends with me?"

"Because we seem to be in the same shoes."

Hearing that, I compare the two of us. We both have a backpack, and always have to pull something with our hand. Travelers like us are quick to recognize other travelers. She gives half her sandwich to Wajo. She seems even more intent on hearing my reason. I can't throw up what I've already eaten, and I don't have a single coin in my wallet, so I'm caught in her snare.

I say in a faint voice, "I do it for freer access."

"The dog is as good an actor as its master," she says, patting Wajo's head as though she were proud.

"Wajo isn't an actor," I say.

"Is that his name, Wajo? So what is he, if not an actor?"

"He really is a guide dog."

"What?"

"He was, at one point."

"Does that mean he isn't anymore?"

"I'm the guide now, and he's the blind one."

"What happened?"

26. My grandfather suffered from diabetes for half his life. And he lived with a visual handicap for one third of that half. It was a formidable disease brought on by complications of diabetes. After losing his sight, he had to resign from his post as an elementary school teacher. His dream had been to be a good father, and to retire as a regular elementary school teacher. My grandfather, no longer able to realize such an ordinary dream, had to stay cooped up in his room, unable to move a step, like an infant. He couldn't believe that he couldn't even use his spoon without help, and cried, "I'm going to kill myself!" every time he lifted his spoon. My grandmother could never keep her eyes off him, for fear that he might do something to harm himself. She had security grilles installed over the veranda windows, afraid that he might jump from the apartment, and put sponges on every corner of the furniture for my grandfather, who was always bruised because he kept tripping.

My grandmother's days were filled with anxiety and difficulties as well. She was no different from my grandfather in that she couldn't take a single step outside the apartment. She herself seemed to have gone blind. After a while, she began to cry, "I'm going to kill myself!" after putting down her spoon, asking what kind of a life hers was to live. My grandfather, afraid that she might do something to harm herself, called out to her every ten minutes, saying, "Malnyeon, are you there?" For him, silence was more awful than darkness. He feared that she'd die before he did. He began to harbor a desire from then on: to be able to take a step out of the apartment without her help. That was the way to save not only himself, but my grandmother as well.

It was two years after he lost his sight that my grandfather finally got Wajo. The two became a perfect team, and spent every day outdoors. From then on, he became the accompanist for a children's service at church, and went to church every day to practice the organ, and went for a walk afterward. That gave him a natural workout, and helped regulate the blood sugar. When I think back now, it seems that he took a walk every day because he wanted to show off that he had such a great dog. Perhaps for that reason, he followed wherever Wajo led, like an unthinking machine. He said it was because he trusted Wajo, but it looked to me as if Wajo had control over him. At times, when trust grows deep, it turns into control.

That's when I first realized that humans can be controlled by animals, too. I feel a little uncomfortable using the word "control," but my grandfather was the first to use the word. "Do you have any idea how I feel? What's the big deal about being controlled, when I can move about as I wish? In this damned house, no one's as good as Wajo!" he'd say. So it was no wonder that he didn't pay attention to the family's advice, that he should be the one to control Wajo. In the end, Wajo really did control everything. Even my heart, which was relieved that now no one would have to die.

27. "According to a witness, Wajo forgot his duty and dragged my grandfather in a completely wrong direction, like he was possessed by something," I said.

"It was a car accident, wasn't it?"

"My grandfather was hospitalized for three months, after which he passed away, and that's when Wajo lost his sight, because of the accident."

"Controlled indeed. How ironic."

My grandfather did not blame or hate Wajo in the least. In fact, he was sad for Wajo, who would have to live out the rest of his life in frustration, just as he himself had, and quietly called to me and said, "You be his eyes from now on." Then a few days later, he gently closed his eyes as though relieved. So ended my grandfather's life, and Wajo's life was changed in an instant. My grandfather and Wajo had been together for eight years.

"I've paid the price for the sandwiches, so I should get going," I say.

I take Wajo's leash and get up from the bench in front of the government office. I throw the sandwich wrapping and the empty Coke can into the trash bin. I feel like I sold a piece of my life for a sandwich. Why do I feel that way, when I could have told her the story without price, as I always did with other people? It's strange, when one of the reasons I came on this journey was because I was dying to talk, and because I wanted someone to talk to me.

I've met countless people, but the woman is a little odd, and has a tendency to be annoying. Maybe I'm just not used to someone like her, who's very forward in asking questions. Still, something is very strange. It feels like the tables have turned somehow. In most cases, I'm the one to initiate a conversation, but now, I'm trying to run away from a conversation. Should I beg for money and pay her back for the sandwich? Debt. That's it. That's why I'm trying to avoid her. I told her my story because I felt like I had to give her something in return. I feel like my story has been exchanged for money.

"You still have to pay me back for the Coke," she says.

I still owe her. To get her money's worth for the Coke, she follows me, noisily pulling her cart and asking me one question after another. She's even noisier than the cart. I wonder if I've ever seemed as noisy as a cart to someone else. Now that I think about it, 201 had said something to the effect. "Your voice is like an empty can. It's loud and noisy, but there's nothing inside. It's like words without meaning! You sound like a kindergarten kid who's out to practice speaking. So stop talking to me!" Maybe that's why I had the hardest time getting 201's address.

The reason why 201 got annoyed was because the conversation we had wasn't quite balanced. Questions should be thrown and received, like a ping pong ball, but because only one side wanted to know about the other, the conversation didn't turn out very well, and the other felt irritated because he had no intention of answering. So applying the same principle, if I asked the woman questions that were difficult to answer, she wouldn't follow me anymore. I turn around, and ask her questions that don't make sense, that are too difficult, or somewhat vulgar. It must be working, because she doesn't say a word. I turn around again.

She says toward the back of my head in an embarrassingly big voice, "I owe you nothing, so I don't have to answer you. But if you'd really like to hear the answers, I'll tell you eventually."

What does she mean, eventually? Will she keep following me? I pick up speed. Her cart seems to pick up speed as well.

"Do you have a place to sleep?" she asks.

I come to a halt at the question. Since I have no money, I can't get a room. Fortunately, though, it's the middle of summer. In summers, we've slept out in the open at a terminal or a subway station, and sometimes on a park bench or under a bridge.

I look down at Wajo. It'd be fine if I were alone, but at times like this, I end up taking a step back, thinking of Wajo. I can't make Wajo, who'd be in his eighties in human years, sleep outdoors. What's more, Wajo isn't the dog he was three years ago.

"There's a motel I know, though it's a little ways from here," the woman says.

"What do you want from me?" I ask.

"I'm observing you."

"Why?"

"For fun."

"I'm not having fun."

"What matters is that I am. I don't care whether you're having fun or not."

"You want to sleep with me?"

"I wouldn't consider that having fun."

That's good. Since I owe her anyway, I decide to borrow just enough money for a room. Since I've already reported my lost card, all I have to do is run to the bank early tomorrow morning and get a new one, and everything will be over.

28. It's not just a little ways to the motel; it's a long ways. I don't know how many crosswalks I've crossed. The woman must be bored, because her questioning resumes.

"Why is he named Wajo?"

She seems to be asking the question, keeping in mind that I still owe her for the Coke. I don't like feeling indebted, so I answer gruffly, "My grandfather named him."

"Does it have a special meaning?"

"My grandfather would mostly say things like '*Iri wajo* (come here)' and '*Dowajo* (help me)' to him; that's how he became Wajo."

"Shouldn't it be Wajueo, since it's *iri wajueo,* and *dowajueo?*"

"You don't get it, do you? It's how the word is actually pronounced. It isn't hard to guess how you did in your Korean classes," I say, revealing my exasperation.

"What do you do for a living?" she asks.

"What do you do?" I return.

"I'm a salesperson, as you saw earlier."

"I'm a letter traveler."

"What a great title. It isn't hard to guess how you did in your Korean classes. That's why you were standing in front of the mailbox. What did you do before, then?"

"Is that the motel?" I ask, pointing to a neon sign, and she grins, looking at it, as she did on the subway.

"Yes. 'The Moon and Sixpence,'" she says.

At that moment, a strange feeling comes over me.

29. As we enter the motel, the proprietor, a man well advanced in years, welcomes the woman. Is she a frequent motel-goer? The two engage in quite a friendly yet serious conversation. A serious conversation with a motel proprietor. It's a very unusual and awkward scene. I take peeks here and there, eavesdropping on their conversation. Contrary to my assumption, it seems that it's been exactly a year since she has come to this motel. They take their time catching up, and then she pays for two rooms.

"The Edward Hopper for him, please," she says.

"That's the first room you stayed in, isn't it?" the proprietor asks.

"I must say, you have a great memory."

"Did you sell a lot of books today?"

"No, not a single one today . . ."

The proprietor nods thoughtfully.

The woman hands me a key, telling me to go up to the second floor. On the key is the name "Edward Hopper," which sounds familiar somehow, instead of a room number.

30. The Moon and Sixpence is a somewhat unusual motel. No, somewhat peculiar. Or you could say it's special, I suppose. It's not a clandestine, immoral place; it looks more like a dormitory. It's a place where you need to be quiet and civilized. The woman explained that it's a special motel that refuses couples and receives only travelers and business guests. When she told me that they don't even sell condoms, the murky city air enveloping me felt sober and clean somehow. I can't quite believe that such a motel exists, but it does, for I've seen it with my own eyes. I've been told that the proprietor is really an artist. That's probably why all the doors of the motel rooms bear a nameplate with the name of an artist, instead of formal numbers. Renoir's room, van Gogh's room, Picasso's room, Klimt's room . . .

The proprietor had long harbored a dream of owning such a motel. A man who ran a motel for a traveler on the road, worn out from fatigue. Perhaps he wanted to restore the true meaning of a motel, which had become tainted. Now that I think about it, his way of dealing with guests did seem different from that of an ordinary motel proprietor. The way he looked at Wajo didn't make me feel uncomfortable at all, and he didn't ask the worn-out question, "Are you here for a rest, or to stay the night?" A quite comfortable and refined motel that did not make a traveler like me feel intimidated or constrained. I don't know why they came to be that way, but motels have a way of making people feel dishonorable, as if they've done something wrong.

The true worth of this motel becomes even more evident when you enter a room. When you open a door bearing the name of an artist, you find that the walls are full of paintings by the artist. You feel as if you're at an art museum in Europe. Even couples burning with lust will have a hard time undoing each other's buttons, with great masterpieces before them. On the bedside table are art books and books on artists, and next to the TV are documentary DVDs on the lives of artists, instead of porn videos. If you stayed in this room for a few days with serious intent, you could probably be on your way again with full knowledge on the artist in question. In short, the motel is wholesome to the point of being boring. The bathroom is equipped with a shower booth instead of a whirlpool tub.

The woman also said that the proprietor remembered the faces of all the guests, even a year after they'd stayed at the motel. She said that that's why she, too, remembered his face and returned. She said that with the right words, you could get a discount on the charge, and possibly, even put it on credit. I wonder if the motel can be sustained when the majority of the customers giving sustenance to most motels are couples who are there for a "rest," but it seems that thanks to regular customers who are reluctant to stay at shady motels, it doesn't suffer a loss. It's at a good location, too, right next to the train station.

31. I'm standing in the middle of the "Edward Hopper Room" recommended by the woman. I grow reverent and solemn, as if I'm at an art museum. Quietly, I take in the paintings on the walls. The paintings make me feel as if there's cold wind blowing in from somewhere, even though it's midsummer. Below the frames are written in detail the titles of the paintings, the years in which they were produced, and the techniques used. The places that serve as backdrops in the paintings are the kind of places that can be commonly seen anywhere in big cities, the kind of places that probably everyone has been to. Hotel rooms, cafes, bars, theaters, gas stations, trains . . .

The cities in the paintings, however, are quite different from the cities I know. Hopper's cities are not boisterous and glamorous, but infinitely empty, eternally bleak, and perpetually silent. People are sitting alone in hotel rooms or cafes, expressionless, reading a book or looking out the window. Even when there are two or more of them, their eyes never meet. All eyes are directed elsewhere, with a certain distance between them. The people do not look comfortable, probably because they're not in the comfort of their home, but are staying briefly in a desolate, external environment. Cities that have lost their sense of hearing, without words, without sounds, and without noise. It seems that in a way, the empty streets and the houses on the hills have been painted without a purpose. That's why the sun shining into the quiet, empty rooms doesn't look warm. It looks as though the sun will be cold when it touches the body. The bleakness felt in the extended space and the loneliness flickering across the faces of the people, their heads bent, seem to be the smallest, as well as the largest, elements the artist could choose to depict solitude.

I browse through the books on Hopper on the bedside table. They say that Hopper, who was born in 1882 and died in 1967, was a major American realist painter. A painter who traveled like me, and did sketches and paintings on the street. Hopper says, "Unconsciously, probably, I was painting the loneliness of a large city." A painter who knew what loneliness was, a painter who for that reason was lonely, a painter who thus had no choice but to paint loneliness.

I look at the paintings again. Hopper was someone who knew what a real city was. He painted real cities. No matter how many people came flocking to the city, and no matter how many people he laughed and chatted and talked with, he could only see one person. That one person, with the same expression on his face and in the same posture, was always looking off in a different direction: out the window, at a book, at a coffee cup, or into himself. He was probably looking at his own self. True loneliness comes not from being alone, but from being with someone else. There didn't seem to be much of a difference between myself, standing in the middle of a motel room, and the figures in Hopper's paintings. Paintings that knew better than anyone where I was at this point in my life. Paintings that resembled me and felt familiar to me. I came on this journey because I was lonely, but I'm still lonely. At that moment, someone flashes through my mind like a lightning bolt.

32. Mother! I thought that the painter's name sounded familiar, and as it turns out, I've seen his paintings in my mother's study.

My mother had a thing for collecting stuff. Just as I began collecting stamps one day, my mother suddenly began to collect things with enthusiasm. My love of collecting comes from my mother. Interestingly, my mother's collection consisted of emotional things, not tangible objects. In other words, she didn't collect things like stamps or model cars, but intangible things like sentences from books, dialogues from movies, or incidents from the news.

When she came home from teaching kids at school, my mother would go into her study and read the paper. She often forgot to cook rice for dinner. When she was done reading the paper, she'd cut out articles with scissors. The cutout scraps went into two different scrapbooks. She divided the paper clippings into two categories: happiness and unhappiness. Every day, she collected happiness and unhappiness, keeping it a secret from her family. I never got a chance to ask her why she did that, but I think she wanted to find out whether there was more happiness or unhappiness in the world. I knew that if she came out of the study looking cheerful, she had collected a little more unhappiness that day, and if she came out looking depressed, she had collected a little more happiness. So on days when there was more happiness, I didn't complain about the food, and tried to help out with the dishes after dinner. Maybe she chose the newspaper because the newspaper is a medium that gets more excited over unhappy incidents than happy ones, I thought.

It was after a certain incident at school that my mother began to collect photographs of paintings. She taught math at a coed high school. She was notorious among the students, who called her "the damned old witch." She put her students in charge during half the class period. All math teachers liked to call up students at random and make them solve problems on the board, but my mother was somewhat malicious. Her malice was directed at students who failed to solve the problems. She had a way of brutally humiliating those who had no mathematical aptitude. She usually made them go outside the classroom and stand there holding up a chair, and in extreme cases, she'd make them go around the other classes during lunch and solve similar problems, and explain the process through which they solved them. She also made them go around the entire school, holding up a sketchbook with the words "I failed to solve a math problem today" written on it.

Then one day, a poor little girl got caught in my mother's snare. The problem the girl had to solve was a very easy one, one that couldn't even be considered a problem, really. But the girl could do nothing more than copy the problem down on the dark chalkboard. My mother got angry. She made the girl go into another classroom and solve the same problem in front of kids she didn't know. The kids all stared at her, with spoons in their mouths. A boy she liked was in that class. The girl was probably so humiliated that she wanted to jump out the window. The boy was probably disappointed to find out that the girl he liked was someone so dumb that she couldn't even solve such an easy problem, and since the other kids all knew about the two of them, he probably wanted to jump out the window, too. The girl ran out of the classroom sobbing. The tears must have blocked her view, for she rolled down the stairs and hurt her head. The girl, who had always been cheerful and vivacious, became a completely different person after that. She lost her temper easily, she didn't laugh, and didn't talk much either. She had wanted to major in art, but she even lost her interest in art. In the end, she decided to transfer to another school.

The day before she left the school, the girl came to see my mother.

She showed my mother, who was sitting in the teacher's room, some paintings one by one and asked, "Do you know who painted these? Do you know what technique was used in this painting? Do you know what style this painting is in? Have you seen a painting like this?" My mother could not answer a single question the girl asked. My mother knew nothing about paintings.

The girl handed my mother all the art books she had brought, saying one last thing. "I didn't know math well, but I did know paintings. But now, because of math, which I didn't have to know, I can't paint, either." After the girl left the school, my mother began to collect paintings instead of unhappiness. Was she, having learned about paintings, a little happier?

33. I take out some writing paper from my backpack. Today, the person I want to write to comes easily to mind. Wajo doesn't bark even once, as if he knows who it is I'm writing.

Dear Mother,

Whenever I think of you, there's always something else that comes to my mind. You always smelled of chalk. Even the food you cooked had that smell. At first I thought it was some kind of a cosmetic product, but I learned, after I entered elementary school, that it was chalk. Being the duty student of the week, I was dusting off the eraser, when the smell of you, Mother, rose up like smoke into the air. That's when I began to have a fondness for chalks, and I would steal them in all different colors and give them to you. When I became good at making stuff, I carved all kinds of animals with them and gave them to you as presents. The problem was that you couldn't keep them for a long time, because they broke and got wet and smashed easily. Later, you scolded me for playing with pencils because for you, chalks were pencils.

I still remember the huge green chalkboard on a wall in your study. You were always standing in front of the chalkboard, solving math problems on it with a chalk and an eraser in your hands. You weren't even aware that white chalk powder was settling down onto your head. When you were having difficulty solving a problem, you'd hold the chalk between your fingers, like a cigarette, and think intently for a while. I still remember clearly how you looked at such moments. The look on your face was like a difficult question, a question that couldn't be answered completely. I thought you looked lonesome and aloof, which is why I began to smoke cigarettes even before Older Brother did. I thought cigarettes held clear answers to the difficult questions in life. And you, Mother, would solve the problems without a hitch after having a smoke. I felt relieved, for some reason, when I heard the sound of the chalk scratch across the board at great speed. As though I were listening to a lullaby. And of course, your face, too, relaxed.

Before you left for work each day, you wrote down three math problems on the board. Older Brother and I, and Jiyun, too, had to solve those problems when we came home from school, before we could eat. You thought it would be embarrassing for the children of a math teacher to be bad at math. But more than that, you believed that all the truth in the world could be found in math. All creations are numbers. That was your philosophy in life. Because of your efforts, we always got good grades at school, as far as math was concerned. Still, I was your least favorite, wasn't I? I always left more problems unsolved than Older Brother and Jiyun.

Did you know? That I pretended I couldn't solve the problems? Why, do you ask? Because I wanted your attention. They say that mothers tend to pay more attention to the stupid child, the slow child. It really worked. You gave me a severe beating whenever I got a problem wrong, but you also gave me that much more attention and instruction. I stayed alone with you in your study, like kids at school who stayed behind after class because they were slower than other kids, and on that pretext, I could chat with you late into the night, and you gave me candy in secret. At the time, I really felt like I was receiving special treatment. But I know in my heart that you were just sad that the child who stuttered was bad at math, too.

Thinking back now, I see that I was the happiest when solving math problems. In math I didn't stutter, and it wasn't frustrating because there was always a clear answer and it was easy. Math gave me the confidence that I could accomplish something without making sounds with my mouth. But more than that, I think you, Mother, were the most difficult problem for me to solve. I even had a hard time calling you "Mother." I had no problem saying the word *father*, so I don't know why the word *mother* was so difficult. During my adolescence, I even imagined that I might not be your son. Maybe it was because I was afraid of you, since you were somewhat cold and adamant, but later on, I felt that I was the only child you didn't like. Frankly speaking, I wasn't a good enough son for you, Mother, who were insatiable. Especially compared to Older Brother or Jiyun. I stuttered on top of that, which must have made me seem stupid.

Now I understand you, Mother. How frustrated you must've been, since you had to decide what my future job would be. I really hated it back then, but now I think that my job, which you chose for me, is just right for me. It's been very helpful in my journey as well.

I learned before I left home that I really was your son, and that you didn't hate me. I saw the scrapbooks in your study. In your desk drawer, there was another file besides the two which held your collections of happiness and unhappiness. In that file, you'd been collecting the happiness of your children. Records of minor incidents in which something good happened to your children, which made you happy. It was Older Brother, of course, who took up the most pages, and then Jiyun. Sadly, there was none on me. I felt bad, but then I saw another file at the bottom. The file, unlike the one divided up between Older Brother and Jiyun, was all for me. There was nothing inside, of course. But I know, Mother, that you, more than anyone else, wanted to put in that file the happiness I brought you. Late as it is, I promise you now, that one day, I will fill up that file.

The motel where I'm staying is quite an interesting place. This room is full of Hopper's paintings. You know Hopper, right? I used to think that his paintings resembled me, but writing this letter, I feel that they resemble you. It's the kind of motel that you should stay at sometime, since you like paintings.

Something you used to say often suddenly comes to my mind. "For you and for others, life begins in joy, but ends in sorrow." When I finish this journey and return home, I'll work hard to live in such a way that your life doesn't end in sorrow. I'll be a son who doesn't stutter, and doesn't seem stupid.

You're probably standing before the chalkboard as usual, solving a difficult math problem. I miss the smell of chalk tonight.

Your son Jihun, from The Moon and Sixpence

34. I put the letter in an envelope, and affix a stamp on the right. A stamp is the cost you must pay to send a letter, and the price paid to the postman for his labor; but to me, it feels like a special symbol. A stamp, to be affixed on the right side of an envelope, is like a heart. A heart that doesn't beat dies, and a letter without a stamp doesn't get delivered. An undelivered letter is as good as dead. This letter, however, has a heart that's beating, like that of a newborn baby, so it will be safely delivered to my mother. I put the letter down on the bedside table, and go into the bathroom.

35. I forgot to buy underwear, so I come out of the bathroom naked again. The paintings in the room make me feel like there's someone else in the room, and I cover the lower half of my body with the towel in spite of myself. I hang the wet underwear on a hanger to dry, and pull the pillow from the bed down to the floor. I'm about to lie down on the floor and put on my earphones when someone knocks on the door.

"Who is it?" I ask, standing by the door.

"It's me," comes the reply.

It's the woman.

"What do you want?" I ask.

"Want a beer?" she asks in return.

"It's too late," I reply.

"Come on, just one?" she persists.

There's no sign that she'll give up. She seems to be implying that since she paid for the rooms, I should do as she wants. If I do drink the beer she offers, what will she demand of me next? She keeps knocking on the door, as though my concerns don't matter at all. It feels like she'll open the door with a key if I don't open it for her. I'm about to open the door, but then turn around in haste. I forgot that I'm naked. That was a close call. I slip on the wet underwear I hung on the hanger, thinking it would be better to wear my own clothes than to wear the robe provided by the motel, and put on some jeans and a T-shirt over it. I feel damp and uncomfortable.

36. The woman walks around the room, sipping her beer, her eyes full of emotion. While looking at the paintings, she steals a glance at the letter I placed on the bedside table. When she's about to reach for it, I firmly stop her.

"Hey!" I yell out.

"Why don't we introduce ourselves? My name is . . ." she begins.

"I don't want to know," I say, because I fear that we really will have to get to know each other once we start calling each other by name.

"What are you going to call me from now on, then?" she asks.

"What do you mean, from now on?"

"It includes tomorrow, for one thing."

I think for a moment and say, "Why don't I call you 751?"

"751 ... That's original. I like it, it's creative. Well, then I'll call you ..." she begins.

"Just call me 0."

"Why 0, of all numbers? Do you like 0?"

"It's a state of nothingness."

"Are you saying that you want to be someone who doesn't mean anything to me, like the number zero?"

"Exactly."

"0 and 751. The numbers are too far from each other. Too much gap between them. Well, I suppose 751 is closer than 752," she says, and laughs cheerfully with her mouth wide open.

For the first time, I take a close look at the woman's face. Her gums don't show. That's the only thing I like about her face. There's something disillusioning about a woman whose gums show when she laughs. When they're overexposed, they even take away the fantasy of kissing. They make a person look like an animal that hasn't evolved enough. But I'm not saying that I want to kiss her or that I like her. It's a very dangerous idea to like someone on the whole just because you like a part of her.

The woman sits down in the middle of the room, and opens a can of beer and hands it to me. My mouth waters in spite of myself. Thinking I'll pay her back tomorrow for everything, since I owe her anyway, I take the beer and sit down. My buttocks feel uncomfortable because of the damp underwear. I gulp down the whole can. The fatigue leaves me, and the discomfort in my buttocks is soon forgotten. The drink makes me feel less guarded toward the woman, and my face is flushed. I want to ask her a question.

"Why did you recommend me this room?" I ask.

"Because you're a traveler," she answers.

I look up at the paintings once again. All the people in the paintings have the look of a stranger to them.

"The artist understands how travelers feel," she says.

"How did you find out about this motel?" I ask.

"A drifter does well to plant a motel in each city. Don't you have a place like that, 0?"

"Not yet. If I did have one, it'd be a place that welcomes Wajo. That's why it seems so unrealistic that a motel like this exists."

"But it is realistic for someone like me. He's going to add two more stories, I hear."

"The business must be thriving."

"Kant's room, Hegel's room, Spinoza's room. It seems that he's going to add philosophers' rooms."

Suddenly, I feel perplexed. Rooms full of books on philosophy? But then it occurs to me that philosophy may be the most suitable subject for a traveler. When you travel, you become philosophical without even realizing it. Even if you don't make a point of creating philosophers' rooms, all the rooms in which travelers stay become philosophers' rooms.

"If it were me, I'd build novelists' rooms . . . A motel where people come to read a single writer's novels. The idea alone is fabulous. Do you have in mind the kind of rooms you'd like to build, 0?"

I think it over. If it were me, I'd build a motel where people feel inclined to write a letter. A motel that sells things you need to write a letter, like envelopes and stamps, and has a red mailbox standing in the lobby. I read an article once, about a study result stating that your health improves when you write letters. In the article, the doctor said that writing letters not only helped students improve their grades, but also had a positive effect on reducing depression and raising immunity level. He also said that writing letters was the simplest way to enhance the quality of life and make people happy. You can believe it, since I myself am an example of the study result. I ignore the look in the eye of the woman, who is waiting for an answer, and say something a little silly.

"A motel with separate entrances for men and women, like a public bath."

"You're still upset? About having a drink with me?" she asks.

"I want to rest," I reply.

"Why do you take Wajo around with you? It must be hard. And he looks pretty old, too," she asks again, eating shrimp chips and sounding as though she herself never gets tired.

I don't know why I keep answering her questions when I'm so tired. It's probably because of the drink.

37. It was never my intention to bring Wajo with me. I took him under my care at my grandfather's request, but I couldn't very well take him on my journey just to fulfill the request. It was obvious that it would be difficult for both of us. Most importantly, I couldn't tell when the journey would end. Having no other choice, I decided to leave Wajo with my grandmother on the day I left on my journey. The dog, however, seemed to have figured out what was happening, and stopped in front of the gate of my grandmother's house and wouldn't budge. I barely managed to drag him into the yard with the help of my grandmother, but it was no use. I kept trying to push him away, but in the end, he bit my pant leg and clung to it. My grandmother tried to pull him away, but she wasn't strong enough. In the end, with my jeans torn, there was nothing more we could do. "He can't help it, it's his nature. Take him with you." Just as my grandmother said, wandering around seemed to be his nature. It wouldn't be easy to abandon a nearly decade-old habit overnight. All the more so, since Wajo is an animal and animals are truer to their nature than humans. My grandmother put in my backpack Wajo's yellow outfit with the words "Guide Dog" stitched on it, saying that there might come a time when we would need it. Wajo was a dog who could survive only by looking after someone as if his own life depended on it. Maybe his nature made him forget the fact that he couldn't see.

38. "How old is he?" the woman asks.

"Thirteen."

"What about you, 0?"

I take a book out of my backpack and read a passage with blurred eyes.

"I put this age as the utmost limit at which a man might fall in love without making a fool of himself."

"Thirty-five?"

"I've got three more years to fall in love without making a fool of myself."

"So you're thirty-two."

"How did you know it was thirty-five, though?"

"It's one of the classics I liked when I was little."

The words make me feel even less guarded toward her.

"That's why you looked so surprised when you saw the motel sign last night," she says.

"I have to admit, I was a little surprised, because that was the book I brought with me when I left home."

"So what are you in search of, away from the comfort of your home?"

"Comfort."

"So are you comfortable now?"

"Somewhat. More than I was at home."

"That's unusual. Don't people usually feel more comfortable at home? How long has it been since you left home?"

"Three years."

"That's a long time."

I myself hadn't thought that this journey would last so long. I'd expected it would take a month or two, at most. It's all because of the letters that the journey has become so prolonged. I'd planned to return home, if only to read the letters that came for me, and to write back. But sadly, not a single letter has come for me yet. So there was no reason yet for me to go home. I refused to give in after a while, thinking, let's see who wins, which was partly the reason why I had come this far.

"What about you, 751?" I ask.

"My journeys are as inconstant as the moon; I don't know when they'll begin and end," she replies.

"Isn't it the moon that matters?"

"The moon? I'm a salesperson, you know. What's important is the sixpence."

"True, if sales is your only motive."

"Are you saying I have an ulterior motive?"

"You started a conversation with me."

"What if that, too, was for sales?"

"Did you follow me to sell a book, then?"

"I can't say no."

"Well, then, you've already suffered a loss. The money you've invested in me exceeds the cost of the book."

"Books can be bought five copies at a time, or even ten."

"Are you asking me to buy ten copies, now? Of the same book? It doesn't matter how great a book is. One copy is enough. It'd be a waste to have several copies of the same book."

"Too many to keep, but not enough to give away as presents."

"The question is, is the book worth giving away as a present?"

"What if it's a book like *The Moon and Sixpence?*"

"I'd buy a hundred, not just ten."

She gulps down her beer; she must be angry that I won't buy her book. She looks somewhat sullen, too. Meanwhile, the underwear beneath my jeans has become dry.

39. Stepping out of The Moon and Sixpence, I go in search of a mailbox as a ritual.

The woman sees the envelope I'm clasping in my hand and asks, "Who's the letter for, and what kind is it?"

"It's a letter saying hello to an acquaintance."

"Do you write letters every day?"

"I do, because mine is a journey of letters."

Today, I spot a mailbox quite easily. I slide the letter in, and immediately start looking around for a phone booth. I don't see one, just as I expected. It seems that I'll have to do a little more walking. The woman looks around, too, and asks me what I'm looking for. I tell her that I'm looking for a phone booth, and she takes out a cell phone from her pocket and hands it to me. I want to accept her offer, for it would make things easy, but decline because it, too, could turn into a debt. Luckily, I see a phone booth in the distance, and make straight for it.

My friend's voice, which I hear at the same time the coins drop, sounds a little sleepy as usual, and he's as irritated as usual as he picks up the phone. Then he comes around and goes on and on about how the "deadly woman" he discovered recently caught him peeping on her, and how he almost became a dead man. It seems, however, that he hasn't given up his peeping fantasy. He even boasts that he'll find an even deadlier woman and be sure to show her to me. I hear him out and hang up.

40. No one wrote me.

41. I see the train station in the distance as I come out of the phone booth. I think it might be a good idea to take the train and go somewhere a little far off. It doesn't matter where. What I've learned on my journey is that the fewer destinations you have, the better. When there's no goal, there's no expectation, and when there's no expectation, there's no disappointment. Freedom is being able to go off when you feel like it. I walk toward the train station. The woman follows me again, pulling her cart.

I turn around and say to her, "Are you going to keep following me, when you don't even know where I'm going?"

"So what if I do? It's not like I have a clear destination. Wherever you go, 0, I can go. Books can be sold anywhere, and read anywhere, too," she says.

Only then do I remember that I owe her. She's saying in a roundabout way that I should pay her back. I veer toward the bank in a hurry, to get my debit card reissued. She follows me to the bank, too. I withdraw some cash with the reissued card, and hand her the money for the room. But she pushes away my hand, saying it isn't money she wants.

Then she says, "You don't seem to understand, but traveling means becoming indebted. You need to know what it means to be indebted so that you can help someone else out. If you must pay me back, you can pay for my room at the next place. It'd be more neat and efficient to pay back for a room with a room, don't you think? If I don't sell any books today, I may not have enough money for a room."

It sounds as though she's asking me to buy one of her books.

"Are you suggesting that we stay at the same motel again?" I ask.

"I guess we should, if you mean to pay me back, right?" she says.

I'm disgusted. I storm out of the bank, and start walking briskly toward the train station as if to run away from her. Suddenly, thick raindrops begin to pour down like a waterfall. The raindrops come pouring down in rough, white streaks, and I can't see what's right in front of me. I run. Wajo runs. The woman runs, too. And the cart runs as well. By the time we get to the station, we look miserable, like drenched little mice that have drowned in water. We look up at the sky through the glass door of the station. The sun is beating down, as if to pretend that it doesn't notice the rain.

I ask the girl at the ticket window for a ticket for the first *Mugunghwa* train. I make the last stop my destination. The woman, who's been standing behind me, gets the same ticket. For the seat next to mine.

42. It's the woman, not me, who loses by buying the ticket, because the seat next to mine is always taken by Wajo before another passenger gets on. As if to prove that, and as if it's the most natural thing in the world, Wajo sits down in her seat, and she looks stunned. She takes another seat without complaint, as if to say that she's giving up her seat only because it's for Wajo. There aren't many passengers since it's a weekday, so she'll be able to sit in comfort for a while. I take out my MP3 player and start listening to music, afraid that she might try to start a conversation. She finally gives up, closes her eyes, and tries to get some sleep.

43. A pop song whose lyrics I don't understand comes flowing out of my MP3 player. Unlike the subway, railroad trains make you think deep thoughts, and bring many people to your remembrance. Most of the time, the thoughts pass by in the form of memories, like scenery passing by outside the window. It's probably because the subway, a transportation for daily endeavors, seems tough and complicated, and railroad trains, a transportation for more romantic pursuits, seem relaxed. There are two people who always come to my mind when I take the train.

109 was someone I often ran into when I took the Honam railroad line. He was a traveling vendor, selling things like snacks, *gimbap,* and regional specialties on a cart. Since I preferred the first seat in the first compartment of the train, or the last seat in the last compartment of the train, I naturally ended up talking to him. He had to replace the items often, so we soon came to know each other over the course of a few railroad trips. It's difficult for people to get acquainted on the train, where countless people get on and off. Our relationship grew to the point where I can say with confidence that 109 and I are acquaintances, because there was the mechanism of "often" between us. I often took the Honam line, and 109 often sold things, pushing the cart. When he had a little time left over after selling his things, he often came over to where I was and struck up a conversation. The conversations that often took place between 109 and me never broke away from certain topics.

"I majored in fashion design. I even worked as a fashion designer at one point," he once told me.

"A fashion designer and a traveling vendor. The gap is too wide, isn't it?" I asked.

"I'm looking for someone."

"Who?"

"There was a girl I loved, but we broke up because of a little misunderstanding. On a train."

"Do you want her back?"

"That's impossible."

"How come? Isn't that why you're looking for her?"

"I'm already married, and I have two beautiful girls."

"Are you telling me that you became a vendor because you just wanted to resolve a little misunderstanding?"

"Because I wanted to live the rest of my life in freedom."

"Whose freedom would that be?"

"Both hers and mine. And maybe the freedom of those around us as well."

"If you find her, then what?"

"I'll be free from this work, and go back to where I was before."

Whenever I got on the train after that, I would first look for 109, even before I found my seat. But gradually, seeing him became less and less pleasant. Seeing him meant that he still wasn't free. But I didn't see him on my last train ride. I remember how I sent him a short letter that day. I don't see him today, either, so I guess he really may have resolved the misunderstanding and found his freedom. I'll be able to confirm my guess through his letter. If he writes me back, I may be able to hear about the "little misunderstanding" that had dominated his life.

44. The other person is none other than my older brother. My brother is the one who got me to go on my first train ride. I think it was his first train ride, too. My brother, who had been lying face down on his bed reading, resting his mind, suddenly jumped to his feet and started putting his on clothes. I felt nervous whenever he did something out of the blue like that. My brother was usually discreet, so when he showed a sudden change in behavior, it meant that he was likely to get himself into big trouble.

He put his hat on, put the unfinished book in his inner pocket, and looked at me, asking, "You want to come with me?"

"D-do you want M-mom to kill you or something?" I said.

"I'll end up killing myself at this rate," he said.

His words terrified me. I hastily put on my clothes and

followed him, afraid that he might die. In other words, we ran away from home. My brother and I got on the train with no destination in mind. My brother, looking at ease as though he were used to taking trains, went on reading his book, and I was absorbed in the scenery outside, natural for someone who had never been on a train before. When the train passed through a dark tunnel, a sound of applause broke out from somewhere. My brother, as though he really had been on a train many times, said that you were supposed to applaud like that when you came across a tunnel. I asked him why, and he said, "Because that's the rule that the majority has established." He himself didn't applaud, though. When I thought about it, it seemed only natural, since he was someone who belonged to the top 0.1%, not even the top 1%, of the Republic of Korea.

Before the tunnel came to an end, he threw the book, whose last page he'd just flipped over, onto my lap and said, "Make sure you read it."

It was *The Moon and Sixpence*. I had a vague idea that the book must have been what led him to come on the train. It was after quite some time that I finally read it.

The railroad trip lasted three days. I began to grow anxious. I'd always known that my brother dreamt of breaking free, but the situation, growing more serious than I'd expected, was giving me indigestion. Nothing I ate on the train tasted good. My brother's prep test was only a few days away.

"Your t-test is coming up soon. Sh-shouldn't we go home?" I said.

My brother said something odd in reply.

"Jihun, do what you want with your life. Understand?"

"What?"

"I'm saying, don't be a top student like me, you ass!"

"W-what's wrong with being a t-top student?"

I'd always envied and been proud of my brother, who was

a top student. I often fell asleep while praying to God in tears that I may be like my brother. My brother wasn't the run-of-the-mill good student. He got the highest score nationwide on every single prep test.

"There shouldn't be any more than one such strange and nasty creature in a family," he said, looking very tired and unhappy, and depraved. I realized then that, thanks to him, I could go on living the way I was. As if I were a little slow. It wouldn't be such a bad thing if I went down a little more, even. A life in which I didn't have to get the highest score. Once I made that resolve, I felt as if I'd passed through a dark and stifling long tunnel. So in a way, my brother saved me on that rocking train, without even knowing the destination.

My brother and I returned home the night before his prep test as if nothing had happened. My mother and father let it pass as if nothing had happened. My brother's first and last act of deviation ended on this somewhat flat note. My brother, of course, got the highest score nationwide on the prep test, as if it were the most natural thing in the world, and no big deal at all. It seemed that on the running train, he had made up his mind to go after success like most people in the world. But he didn't read any more novels after that. *The Moon and Sixpence* was the last novel he ever read.

45. Big cities become big cities because there are a lot of people and buildings in them. Arriving in a big city full of people and buildings, the train itself becomes a big city. The person who bought the ticket for the seat in which the woman is sitting must be a resident of a big city, too, or someone who came to visit a big city for a little while. The woman, who yields her seat to the person, goes to the bathroom compartment, pulling her cart. I feel bad for some reason, as if I've robbed her of her right. I go after her, taking Wajo with me. Actually, I feel more comfortable in the bathroom compartment when I'm traveling with Wajo on a train. It's easier to put up with the dirty looks of the passengers and the train crew in the bathroom compartment.

The train passes through a big city. The woman, standing on a step of the entrance staircase with her arms crossed, looks out the window with a sullen expression on her face. I'm not sure if she's mad at me, or is just absorbed in the scenery. As the train enters a tunnel, she yawns lazily. Suddenly, an image of her selling books on the subway comes to my mind. Along with the image comes the question I had on my mind at the time.

"Why do you sell books? When there are so many other things?" I ask.

"Because they're books," she says, without turning her eyes away from the window. She still looks sullen.

"Why don't you sell more than just one, when you're selling them anyway?" I ask.

"Because it's my book," she replies.

"I'm sure it's your book, 751."

"I mean, I wrote it."

"Huh?"

I take a book from her cart, and compare the profile photo to her face. In a way, they look similar, but in away, they don't. In the photo, she isn't wearing glasses, and looks like a different person because it's been Photoshopped. So has she been following me because she's a writer? I mean, writers by nature like to observe, pry, and meddle. And they love to use what they learn in their writing.

"I can't tell at all with the photo," I say.

"Photographs are deceiving. They don't perfectly reflect the reality," she says.

"Why did you say you were a vendor?"

"There's nothing wrong with what I said. After all, novelists are vendors who have to sell their novels. They have to write good novels and raise their brand value to make them sell. The only difference is that they disguise their products as art."

"You know that's not what I mean. I mean, why are you personally selling your own novels? Bookstores will do that for you."

It seems that selling your own novels would be as difficult as selling your own body. If I said that, she'd probably say, how is it any different from selling the bread you baked, or the *gimbap* you made? But no one wonders, as they buy it, who made that *gimbap*. *Gimbap* is something you're supposed to make and sell yourself. But novels are different. People think novels should be sold by someone else in order for them to maintain their dignity. The more commercial art becomes, the more it is accused of being vulgar. Who, indeed, would write novels if they had to sell their own?

In a way, I do wonder what the difference is between novels and things such as bracken and mackerels sold at the marketplace. There was a day when art was considered vulgar. If art isn't considered vulgar today, it's probably because at some point, it began to elevate itself and receive noble treatment, and naturally became haughty. After all, what the woman is doing isn't all that different from what a famous author does, having a book signing at a large bookstore. A bookstore, in the end, is a somewhat refined marketplace. You can't sell your own works without being passionate about yourself. The woman is more courageous and less hypocritical than those who neglect their own works, turning them into rubbish. Instead of asking her, I take another look at the profile. *Toothpaste and Soap* is her third full-length novel.

"A long time after my first novel came out, I went to the bookstore feeling excited. It's thrilling to see your books on display at the bookstore. But no matter how hard I looked, I couldn't find my book. So I asked an employee, who checked on the computer and told me that there were some copies in stock in the warehouse, and went to get them. So my books, not even two months after publication, had been removed to a dark warehouse. If they were on display where they could be seen, even a reader who didn't know about me would be able to find them, but if they were stuck in a warehouse like that, only those who knew about me could buy them, by asking an employee. That's the system they have at bookstores," she said.

"So you lost faith in bookstores, is that it?" I asked.

"You could say that. I also thought, of course, that it'd be a novel attempt for an author to personally sell her own books," she answered.

If she became a bestselling author, the novel would become a commercial product, not just a work of literature, so it would be easy to find it at little neighborhood bookstores and even discount stores. Then you wouldn't have to go through such hassle to buy it. I can finally understand why she said she wanted to build a motel with novelists' rooms. She wanted to become a famous author and have such a room. I think about it: a bookstore that doesn't display a single copy of your book, and a novelist's room that displays nothing but your books.

"If you become a bestselling author, then what?" I ask.

"Even if that happens, I'd still go around selling them," she says.

Her answer takes me by surprise.

"Why? You'd be able to have faith in bookstores then," I ask.

"At first I did it because I didn't have faith in bookstores, but that's not the only reason anymore," she replies.

"What other reason is there?"

"I just like to go around meeting people. It's even better when I meet someone who buys my books, and I also like to sign my own books."

Suddenly, I'm curious about her book.

"Why eat toothpaste and soap?"

"If you're curious, buy it and read it."

The sullen expression on her face never leaves.

46. We get off in a small town near the sea. Though it's a small town, we find the station square swarming with people as we come out. Whenever the wind blows, the salty smell of the sea and the smell of seafood come rushing in. The woman stops in her tracks at the center of the square and looks around. She seems to be looking for a spot in which to sell her books. She walks toward a wooden bench next to a streetlamp. Then she jumps up on the bench with her shoes on and begins to play the harmonica. The music sways the heart. Drawn to the sound of the harmonica, people gather one by one around the bench. They are like a swarm of mosquitoes, blindly rushing toward the light of a streetlamp in midsummer. They all look like people whose train hasn't arrived, people who have nowhere special to go, or people who have just gotten off the train. When a number of people have gathered, the woman displays her books as she did on the subway, advertising them. The people look a little nervous, not the way they looked when they were listening to the sound of the harmonica. People who rush in blindly tend to turn around mercilessly when they find out what is wanted. She was just trying to sell something, they say, and go into the station with indifference, looking as though they've been betrayed by someone they trusted. Some people throw us a few coins, thanking us for the music, and get on their way. The people who had gathered around leave one by one. In the end, just the two of us remain.

The key, therefore, lies in not having people gather blindly. Her sales tactic seems somewhat problematic. People feel tricked because she lures them in with music, and then pulls her books out.

"How can we get people interested?" I ask.

" . . . "

"I asked you earlier, didn't I? Why the narrator eats toothpaste and soap. Do you remember what you said?" I ask again.

"If you're curious, buy it and read it," she recalls.

"Bingo! That's it. We have to pique their curiosity," I say.

"How?" she asks.

"Mark your books and have them take a look. Pick out the sentence you're the most proud of, sentences you like the most, and dialogues or paragraphs that can trigger their curiosity," I say.

She's hard at work leafing through the book. Once again, she begins to gather people by playing the harmonica. Little by little, people come flocking once again, though fewer in number than before.

47. I sit down on the bench with my legs crossed in a refined, elegant way. Then I put the book on my lap and read to the audience. The woman continues to play the harmonica next to me, very quietly. The music is just at the right volume that it doesn't interfere with either the reading or the listening. My reading begins with the provocative, perplexing sentences, "Today, I ate toothpaste. Tomorrow, I will eat soap." The people perk up their ears at that first sentence alone. Their faces seem to be asking, why would someone eat such things? And they continue to pay attention.

I read with great care the sentences the woman has picked out. I don't stutter, and I don't make a single mistake. My pronunciation couldn't be more clear and precise. I clearly emphasize parts that should be emphasized, and I put emotion into parts that need to be emotional. The atmosphere grows quite serious, and the people fall deeper and deeper into her sentences. The sentences trigger the audience's curiosity, and my clearly pronounced words prick their ears like thorns.

When the reading is over, there's applause everywhere. I introduce the woman to the audience, telling them that she's the author of the book. The audience is even more intrigued, and there's another round of applause. Someone raises his hand high and asks the woman a few questions, and the woman, looking a little shy, answers the questions. When the question and answer session is over, people who want to find out why the narrator eats toothpaste and soap buy some books. The woman signs the books with a flair. In this way, people who remember her name and her sentences get on trains headed to different cities. They won't forget her, not even in those cities.

48. "How come you're so good at reading?" the woman asks.

The woman, who had been looking sullen the whole time before we arrived in the small town, finally looks a little touched. I tell her that I'm good at reading because it's something I've been doing since I was little.

"They were my words, but they didn't sound like my words; they sounded pretty decent. What's your secret?" she asks.

Like the words of an author who said that writing becomes a temptation to someone who can't speak, someone who can't speak articulately is also tempted to write. They can't help it. Having given up on speaking freely with people, I resorted to written words. Written words made me feel comfortable, and naturally, I began to spend a lot of time reading or writing. Mostly, I read novels and poetry, and when there was something I wanted to say to someone, I always wrote a note instead of making a phone call. Whenever I was reading, I made an effort to read aloud if possible. When I read aloud, I felt as though I were listening to the words spoken by someone else, and also as though I were talking to someone. When I read books out loud, I stuttered a little less than I did when I was speaking. I became disciplined enough later that I didn't stutter at all, at least not when I was reading books. Written words are laid out in advance, so there's no pressure. Ideas flowed easily in the form of writing, no matter what kind of writing it was, and words flowed easily when I wrote down those ideas. I believed that someday, I would be able to speak with words flowing out of my mouth like that. And just as I believed, I can now speak with the words flowing out of my mouth. Like the cry of a newborn baby, my words came spilling out all at once when something tapped me on my buttocks. Once my words came spilling out, I could no longer stay at home, for I felt stifled there.

"You're telling me that you used to stutter? That's a lie. Who'd believe that after hearing you read the way you just did?" she says.

Sometimes, I wish it were all a lie, too. I wish it were a lie, when I want to go back to the time before my words came spilling out. To be honest, this is the first time I've read before the public. I'd only read aloud by myself, hiding in a small room.

49. The woman says that she'll treat me to dinner. This time, I feel that there's a good enough reason to accept the offer, so I follow her without complaint. Walking ahead, she enters a pretty big family restaurant in front of the station. It feels as though we have become a family. But it must be a little too early for us to be acknowledged as a family. We're held back at the entrance by an employee. It's because of Wajo.

The woman pleads with the employee, but to no avail. The employee, too, pleads with the woman, saying that the customers won't like the dog. It seems almost as though they'll even give us money to leave. The woman explains that the dog is tame and clean, as you can see, but it's no use. In the end, she even begins to scold the employee. Now that I think about it, she's a bit quick-tempered, and quite aggressive. At her violent protest, the employee comes up with a compromise and tells us to keep Wajo tied outside and go eat, just the two of us.

I watch in silence to see how their argument will turn out. I feel indifferent, because I'd expected as much. This country is not friendly enough to dogs to allow them into restaurants. Dogs would probably not be welcome even at restaurants that serve dog meat. For that reason, the kinds of places we prefer has naturally come to consist of takeout restaurants, McDonald's, and street snack stalls. But once in a while, I crave something other than fast food, something served in a restaurant, something like the food my mother cooks. Especially when it's cold or raining. There is a way, of course.

50. I drag the woman out, and enter an alleyway with no one else around. As she watches, I put on my sunglasses and take out the fluorescent outfit to put on Wajo. Excited, she snatches the outfit from me and puts it on Wajo herself. With a look on her face that says she understands me at last, she searches for my eyes beyond the dark sunglasses. For a brief moment, our eyes meet through the black barrier.

Once again, we challenge ourselves to "eating at a restaurant." This time, we choose a *samgyeopsal* restaurant. Just as we expected, it isn't easy. The proprietor doesn't look too happy. This time, he seems more displeased with me, a blind man, than with Wajo, disguised as a guide dog. It goes to show that an outfit alone can create misconceptions about people and dogs, and that misconceptions can change in an instant. I feel bitter that we need the permission of a restaurant proprietor just to eat a single meal, but the cooperation of a normal person is required for an abnormal person to live like a normal person. In order not to be denied, excluded, rejected, and shut out. While the proprietor hesitates, the woman steps forward and speaks up in a sharp voice. This, too, can be considered cooperation of a normal person.

"You do know about the Disabled Welfare Act, Article 45, Clause 2, which states that if you deny the entrance of a guide dog for the disabled, you must pay a three-million-won fine, don't you?" the woman says.

Humans are animals that cower before legal clauses. They can make them obey. The proprietor is unable to say anything, like a dog with its tail down. We are admitted without a problem, thanks to the woman who stated the clause with finesse.

Sitting without reserve and without discrimination, I ask, "Was that clause for real?"

It must have been, since you'd have to know a lot to write a novel.

"Not at all, actually. You have to be an accomplished liar to write a novel," she says shamelessly.

But thanks to the accomplished lie of the novelist, we can eat our fill of sizzling *samgyeopsal.* Wajo, too, has his fill of meat, for the first time in a while. It even occurs to me that I should take advantage of that clause, too, somewhere down the road.

"Repeat that clause," I prod the woman.

"What did I say . . ." she says, making an effort to remember as she turns over the meat.

In this world, lies go over better than the truth more often than not. Lies set your mind at unease, but your body at ease. And so we finish our meal at ease for the first time in a while.

51. Having filled our stomachs, we head toward the motel. My body is shivering and I feel a cold coming on. It's best to stay out of showers, and I shouldn't have rushed so.

"Is there a motel you know?" I ask, my teeth chattering.

"This is my first time here, too. So we should stay at the same motel, right? You freaked out at the idea before," she says.

I clam up. It seems that tonight, we should just pick any motel. Even though all motels look pretty much the same, it isn't easy to get rid of the compulsion to choose and decide.

The receptionist at Motel Arabian takes out a key as we enter.

Then he rubs the key holder with his thumb, as though it's a magic lamp, and asks, "Are you here for a rest, or to stay the night?"

We must look like a couple. I ask him for two rooms, and he seems to think that we're using separate rooms because we had a fight. I pay for the woman's room as well as mine. Thus I settle all my debts.

52. The sign reads "motel," but inside, it looks more like a shabby inn. The ambience and the furniture layout make me feel as though I'm back in the motel I stayed at a month into my journey. I hadn't been feeling well back then, either. Traveling was a lot more of a strain than I'd imagined, and I was having my first crisis since I set out. To overcome the crisis, I downed two bottles of *soju* I'd bought at a convenience store without anything on the side. The drink spread through my veins like poison. I felt drained in an instant, and my mind seemed to scatter like grains of sand in a desert. I felt out of it, and extremely depressed.

In a state of extreme tipsiness and depression, I made a decision as to whether or not I should continue with my journey. As soon as the decision was made, all kinds of other decisions regarding life came rushing at me, as though they'd just been waiting for the chance. In the end, I was led to the ultimate question of whether or not I should continue to live. For a brief moment, I felt acutely how unbearably painful life was, and felt that everything was futile. Suddenly, I really wanted to die. Later, another self within me made the impulsive decision to die, all by himself.

Following the order in my head, I got to my feet, reeling as I did. I fastened dusty shoelaces to a rod on the wall, where you were supposed to hang clothes. To make sure that the rod was sturdy, I even tried pulling it out. It was sturdy. It didn't seem likely that the rod would break or fall in the process. A failed suicide attempt would only bring deeper humiliation. Everything was ready now, so it would all come to an end when I put my neck in the right spot, lightly and simply as if hanging a hat on a nail.

I took a deep breath, and put my neck through the loop. The earth, as though it had been waiting for the opportunity, pulled me down to the floor with all its might. I felt great pressure as though the shoelaces were cutting my throat. So this is what it feels like to choke, I thought. I wanted to die with dignity, but I must have been in a little pain, for my legs flailed around and I began to cough. Wajo heard the sound and began to bark. Little by little, I began to lose my consciousness. It felt blissful in a way, and also as if I were dreaming. Tens of thousands of thoughts and memories of things that had happened squeezed their way into that brief, confused moment, like shattered fragments of film.

At that moment, I saw my flushed face on the vanity mirror across from me; I was about to die. Beneath my reflection, I also saw Wajo, barking with his tail down. What would happen to the blind dog if I died here? He'd get sold off to some strange place, get beaten by nasty people, or starve to death out on the street while wandering around strange places. This thought suddenly pierced my mind. Then I seemed to sober up a little. And in that moment, I saw the face of my grandfather, who had asked me if, after he passed away, I would care for Wajo. The faces of my family flashed through my mind one by one, vanishing like clouds. In the meantime, my reflection in the mirror was growing more and more ghastly.

Wajo seemed to sense the gravity of the situation, for he bit one of my flailing feet and wouldn't let go. It seemed that he was trying to pull me down. The more I struggled, the more fiercely he bit. My flesh got torn, and blood dripped to the floor. When I came to, I was lying on the floor. The earth had pulled me down. Still hanging on the rod were the dirty shoelaces, dangling there where my neck should have been. Perhaps it was Wajo who had pulled me down.

53. One prevents the suicide of another, who then prevents the suicide of yet another. If I'd died back then, if the earth and Wajo hadn't worked together to stop me, I wouldn't have been able to save another. I put the shoelaces, which had choked my neck, back on my sneakers, and left the motel the next day. What I was wearing were not sneakers, but a pair of deaths. Whenever the thought occurred to me that two deaths were weighing down on my feet, I felt a desire to walk more, and with each step I took, I seemed to move further and further away from death.

One day, when I thought I'd moved very far from death, I met a man on a bridge. 32, the man, had taken his sneakers off and placed them neatly side by side, and was about to go up on the rail. I ran toward him with all the strength I had. One pair of deaths was running in order to save another pair of deaths. I barely managed to grab his arm and jerk it back. If I'd arrived just a second later, his body would have become food for the fish. Barely having escaped death, he gasped for breath. I, too, gasped as I stared at him, who had just escaped death. The look on his face said that a failed suicide attempt doesn't bring humiliation, but a changed perspective on the world.

We sat side by side for a long time on the bridge. I told 32 about my suicide attempt at the motel. I also told him how, whenever I looked down at my sneakers, I wanted to run far away from death. When I said that, he stared fixedly at my shoelaces.

Then he said, "Would you trade shoelaces with me?"

"Shoelaces, not sneakers?" I asked.

I hesitated at first because it was an unusual suggestion, but in the end nodded my head in consent. We immediately traded our shoelaces. 32's shoelaces were fluorescent. They looked a little awkward on my white sneakers, but I didn't think they looked bad. My soiled laces made his clean sneakers look dirty at once, but he didn't seem to think they looked bad, either. We parted ways on the bridge. I turned around slightly and saw him walking briskly, looking down at my shoelaces from time to time. At that moment, I felt with all my heart that I was lucky to be alive and not dead. The earth and Wajo had saved not just one life but two, and in the end, dozens of lives.

54. My body is covered with red spots. I feel like just crawling into bed. But I can't, for I know all too well that even if I did, I wouldn't be able to fall asleep. A habit that has been a part of you for a thousand days cannot be abandoned because of just one case of cold. The red spots might subside after I finish writing a letter.

I lie face down on the bed with a blanket wrapped around me, and barely manage to pick up a pencil. The lead, however, is broken. I take out a pencil sharpener from my backpack and rotate the pencil. Wood shavings come rolling up like lace. To be honest, pencils are something of a hassle at times like this. Still, I always stick to pencils when it comes to writing letters. Pens make me nervous, because errors can't be erased. Pencils always forgive you even when you make mistakes. Completely, too. So letters should be written in pencil. That's my long-held belief.

Dear Father,

I got caught in the rain today and have come down with a bad cold. Maybe that's why I felt prompted to write you. I can just about imagine what you'd say if you saw me. Stupid boy! You caught a cold in the middle of the summer, when even a dog doesn't. Tsk-tsk. And then you'd go down to your basement laboratory, where no light comes in, and make something in the blink of an eye, as if by magic. As if only making something would solve the problem.

You were always that way, Father. The greatest of your inventions were all created when there was a serious or ugly problem at home. They were like mold, feeding on the unhappy energy of our family. There were too many of them, almost grossly so, to call it a coincidence. From some time on, I began to feel uncomfortable about even touching your inventions, because there was something disturbing about them. As the mold multiplied, I loathed you more and more, Father, so that I could hardly bear it. I also thought you were incompetent. I resented you for not being able to handle even a single problem at home as the head of the family.

I thought you had a list of things to invent written out in advance, and took them from the list and made them one by one whenever a problem arose. I thought they were excuses for you to get yourself out of vexing problems. You shut yourself up in your laboratory and struggled with dozens of designs until you succeeded.

Whenever you came running out of the laboratory, with your invention in hand and shouting "Eureka!" the problem would already have been completely worked out by Mother and the three of us. Do you know what occurred to me later, even? That you wanted something bad to happen at home, so that you'd be able to invent something great. Because that's what gave you the ability to concentrate on your research. As a result, each of the inventions that have brought you renown has a story behind them.

I confess at last, I was the one who broke the ventilator you built with great ambition, to submit to the Geneva International Invention Exposition. Older Brother knew, but he took the blame for me. I remember how you beat him to a pulp. He lost two of his front teeth, which made him look like an idiot. I thought since you loved him so much, nothing would happen if he said he was the one who broke it. That morning at dawn, I saw you crying for the first time. Do you remember what you said when I went into the laboratory? You said that the ventilator wasn't just a ventilator, but his heart.

It was when Older Brother was undergoing a heart surgery that the design for the ventilator was completed. You believed that the reason why the surgery went successfully was because you had completed the design. Then you told me about each of the inventions you had come up with up to that point. Things that were created when Mother was facing the risk of expulsion from school, when Jiyun was getting her nose job, when Grandfather lost his sight, when I was taking my college entrance exam ... I learned at last that there was a subtitle for each of the inventions. You remembered everything, even the little things that the rest of us had forgotten, as though you had worked out all the problems at home by yourself. As I thought about it, I realized that the problems that were at hand when you had succeeded in creating your inventions had all been successfully resolved. Older Brother's heart, too, was beating without a problem, thanks to the ventilator. It was a magic spell that was yours alone.

To you, Father, invention was like cooking. Just as Mother cooked up food in the kitchen, you came up with the most fantastic things in the basement as though you were cooking. It seemed that to you, inventing something was as simple as frying an egg. There was nothing you couldn't make at our request, and nothing you couldn't fix. Thanks to you, Father, we were able to lead a comfortable life. When you quit your job as a physics teacher and declared you were going to be a full-fledged inventor, you persuaded Mother with the sweet words that you'd make a robot to clean for her. Until you succeeded in making such a robot, of course, you had to serve as one yourself. You were pretty good at cooking, too, probably because you were someone who invented things the way people cooked. This is a secret, but you were better at cooking than Mother was.

And how fantastic were the toys you made. They were special, on an entirely different level from the plastic toys that other kids played with. Your airplanes flew in the sky, your cars ran on the highway, and your rockets were launched far out into outer space. They were all one of a kind, and so I, too, could be one of a kind. Thanks to that, I passed my childhood without much trouble. I know, of course, that you made more toys for me than for Older Brother, and better ones, too, because I stuttered.

I remember what you said in an interview with

a science magazine. When asked what your greatest invention in life was, you answered without hesitation that it was your three children. Jiyun, being immature, grumbled saying that you should've done a better job of inventing your only daughter and youngest child, but she'll mature as she grows older. Reading the interview, I can't tell you how proud I was to be your son. I'm sure that Older Brother and Jiyun feel the same way.

Will you make me something great, Father, so that I may return home safely after this journey? Knowing you, I think you might be waiting for me with something already prepared. I can't wait to go and see what it is. I'm sure that your magic spell will work as always, Father. Maybe it's working already, because I seem to be feeling a little better. Take care you don't catch a cold, Father. The basement at home is unusually cold, even in the middle of summer. I'll write again.

Your son Jihun, from Motel Arabian

55. There's something that my inventor father always used to say. "The past is always consecrated for the present, and the present is always sacrificed for the future." Just as the words say, the today that is sacrificed will make tomorrow shine brightly. Thinking that, I put the letter in an envelope and seal it.

56. My eyes open slightly, as though in a dream, at the sound of knocking on the door. My mind is so confused that I can't tell whether it's a dream or reality. My whole body is drenched in sweat, and I can't move at all even when I try to raise myself up, as if I'm having a terrible nightmare. I want to speak, but no words come out. The sound of knocking comes again, faintly. Who's disturbing someone else's sacred sleep in the middle of the night? It must be a guest staying in another room, who has come to the wrong door. Thinking he'll leave soon, I pull up the blanket over my head with heavy hands and try to go back to sleep. But this time, I hear the sound of a key unlocking the door. And then the person bolts in through the door and shakes me awake. Startled by the forced entry, I leap up from the bed as though the shackles that had been binding me have come undone. I can't tell who the intruder is because of the dazzling light. Only after a while can I make them out: the receptionist and the woman.

"You startled us. Are you all right?" the receptionist asks.

I was the one who was startled, and I'm not all right.

I rub my eyes and ask, "It's the middle of the night—what's going on?"

"It's time for you to check out, but we didn't hear you getting ready, so we wondered if . . ." the receptionist trails off.

"Time to check out?" I ask.

I narrow my eyes and look at my watch. It's well past noon. I'd slept in, unaware of the sun, high in the sky. The woman looks quite shaken, too, and the receptionist looks at me with great relief on her face. Then she says that she'd been paying us extra attention because she sensed something odd when we got separate rooms. It seems that there had been several accidents at this motel. She asks me to check out and returns to the desk. I'm so shaken that I feel drained, and can't even stay sitting up. I collapse back onto the bed.

"Aren't you going to check out?" the woman asks.

"I don't think I should today. I've come down with a cold. I'm feeling a little better than I did yesterday, but it might last longer if I strain myself."

"How bad is it?"

"What, are you going to get me medicine or something?"

"Yeah."

"Thanks, but it's okay. I'll be all right if I rest for a day. You could send this off for me, though," I say, handing her the letter I'd placed at my bedside.

"Oh, I need to make a phone call, too. No, I'll do that myself later. In any case . . ."

"Could you buy something for Wajo to eat on your way back? Here's my wallet," I say.

She takes the wallet, and takes her cell phone out of her pocket and hands it to me. For a moment, the cell phone seems like the most wonderful, convenient thing in the world. It is like the temptation of the serpent. Should I take it, or shouldn't I? Taking courage from what she said about traveling meaning becoming indebted, I take it in the end. She leaves the room.

Panting for breath, I call my friend.

He says in a wide-awake voice, "Why are you moaning? You're not doing a live broadcast, are you?"

"I'm not in the mood to joke around."

"Hey, I've never seen this number before. Did you get a cell phone?"

I don't have strength enough to speak, so I get down to the point, and hang up.

57. Just as I expected, no one wrote. As usual.

58. My eyes fly open at the sound of the woman opening the door and coming in. As soon as she enters, she says she walked for a very long time because she had difficulty finding a mailbox, and hands me a packet of medicine and asks me how I'm feeling. She's like a mother. Now that I think about it, she seems like a pretty decent person. She takes out some food from a sack and spreads it out on the floor, saying that people should eat well when they're sick. There's food for Wajo, of course, plus steaming bowls of rice and takeout soup and stew from a restaurant. I feel as though I've been invited to a feast. Feeling in a rush, I'm about to pour the medicine into my mouth when she takes the packet away.

"Don't you know that you're supposed to take medicine after a meal?" she says.

She lifts the blanket off of me, forces me to sit up, and leaves the room. The smell of the food stirs up my appetite. My mouth waters, and I feel invigorated. I eagerly wield my chopsticks as though I've been starving for days. I did skip a few meals, after all. Wajo, too, wolfs down his share in the blink of an eye. Only after the frantic binge does it occur to me that I haven't even said a word of gratitude to the woman. Should I have left some food for her? The Styrofoam dishes are spotless, as though they've been licked clean.

59. I've taken the medicine and am putting the empty dishes away when the woman comes in again. But she isn't just coming in. She's moving into my room, bringing all her stuff with her.

The receptionist pokes her head in behind her and says, "You should've done that from the beginning. You're staying just till noon tomorrow, right?"

I tell her yes, for now. The receptionist curls her lips, certain that we're a couple and had used separate rooms only because we'd had a fight. The woman must have read the same look on the receptionist's face, for she starts to rattle off what sounds like excuses that I may not feel offended.

"I thought it made sense to share a room since I don't have enough money for a room. We're not a couple anyway, so it doesn't matter, right?"

For a moment, I find myself questioning her kindness earlier on. She hadn't brought me food and medicine without reason. Still, I can't be heartless and tell her to get out of my room right now. I'm not so shameless that I can just ignore her kindness, and I understand her situation well enough as a fellow traveler. We're not a couple anyway, so nothing would happen between us, and assuming that nothing happens, there's no problem sharing a room. It would be senseless for us to use separate rooms, when we're travelers who can't afford to waste a single coin. Besides, this room is big and spacious enough for two people to share, so we can't use the excuse that it's too small.

A problem to be solved must be viewed from different angles. It may not be all right, precisely because we're not a couple. No, regardless of whether or not we're a couple, I don't understand how the woman and I have come to share a room. We've probably come to this point by taking turns owing each other and paying each other back.

She seems to sense that I feel uncomfortable, for she says in a small voice, "I'll stay quietly by Wajo."

60. The woman, who has been sitting quietly next to Wajo, takes a twelve-inch laptop out of her backpack. While waiting for it to start up, she takes a charger out of her backpack, plugs it in into an outlet, and puts her cell phone on it.

She checks the charger to see if the red light is on, and checks on me, asking, "Don't you want desperately to be home when you're sick? Why don't you go home, if it's too much to bear?" she asks.

"I can't," I say.

"Don't you have a home?"

"Being sick isn't reason enough to go home."

I wrap the blanket around myself like a cocoon.

"What would be reason enough to go home?"

"A letter."

"A reply, you mean?"

I nod my head quietly.

"You haven't gotten a single reply yet?" she asks.

Again, I nod my head quietly. She looks a little surprised.

"Do you write every day?" she asks.

"Sometimes I can't, but I try to write every day. Like in a journal."

"You must have more friends than meets the eye, since you have so many people to write."

"What?" I demand sharply.

"All right, I'm sorry. I'm sure you don't write the same person every day, so who do you usually write? Friends? A girlfriend?"

I wasn't going to answer, but change my mind.

"I write 2, I write my family, I write 149, I write my friend, I write 327, I write my co-workers, and I also write 502. I write someone different every day," I say.

When the laptop has booted up, the woman puts her fingers on the touchpad and moves the cursor. When she clicks a file in a yellow folder, quiet and serene New Age music flows out. I begin to relax. Next, she hooks up her digital camera to the laptop and transfers the photos she took today to the hard drive. Then she gets on the Internet. She continues to ask me questions while staring into the little screen.

"The numbers you just listed. They have something to do with the number 751, don't they?" she asks.

"Yeah."

"I was curious. I thought there must be some kind of a law or principle, even if there's no meaning. How are they related to you, 0? Are they people you met while traveling?"

"Yeah."

"So I'm the 751st person you've met?"

I nod.

"So I'm the last one so far, aren't I?"

"I can't wait to meet the next number. It might be a beautiful girl. Someone I'm destined to meet."

"Or it could be a notorious murderer," she says, lifting her shoulders slightly as though she has goose bumps.

"Do you have to say things like that?"

"You should talk."

"Huh!"

"Why do you put numbers to people? People aren't cars, you know."

"Numbers are easy to remember, convenient, and don't overlap since they're infinite, and they're automatically put in order. Same names may exist, but not same numbers."

"To me it seems harder. Aren't names easier to remember?"

Ever since I was little, I've always been good at numbers and liked numbers, probably because I take after my parents. In addition, I have an excellent memory and remember perfectly everything I've seen. In particular, I have an extraordinary ability to memorize and recall anything with numbers. Even my brother, considered a prodigy, did not have a memory that surpassed mine. That's when I felt for the first time that God was fair. I wasn't able to speak without effort, but I could remember things without effort. But when I tried to put the things I remembered effortlessly into effortlessly spoken words, my mind became muddled before I knew it, and I couldn't say anything at all. Remembering something and putting what I remembered into words were different things altogether, belonging to different realms.

The reason why I like numbers is because numbers, at least, don't lie. They have a clear, definite, sure answer. They don't make you suspect anything else. That's why I have a habit of reducing everything to a number and calling it by that number. Something that's been reduced to a number can never be forgotten. Things that can't be forgotten don't betray or lie, at least not while they remain unforgotten. If people can call everything by a number or explain everything through a number like I do, there will be no misunderstanding or misperception. If to everyone father was 1 and mother 2, older brother 3 and younger sister 4, no one would expect or demand of them anything more than the numbers. But because they were never 1 or 2, they had no clear answers. So even if you lived with them all your life, you couldn't understand them, and they didn't give you any answers. Things will probably remain the same in the future. For they couldn't be called by a number, and neither should they.

"That reminds me of something a physicist said. That if an entire book were written in numbers, it would be the truth. If, like you said, 0, a desk was called 12, and a cat 45, language wouldn't be necessary, would it?" the woman says.

"I don't mean it wouldn't be necessary, I mean the numbers would be a language in themselves. A universal language."

"You've met only 751 people in three years?"

"What do you mean, only? To me, they're as many as the stars. I don't grant a number to just anyone."

"What kind of a person would you have to be?"

"Someone who tells me their address."

If I counted all the people I've met so far, the number would be well over three or four times 751. Of all those people, there were seven hundred and fifty who told me their address when I asked them in the final moment. When I asked people for their address, the first thing they did was become suspicious. Then gradually, they would become guarded. Even those I thought I'd gotten to know well through conversation turned into completely different people when I asked them for their address. It seemed as if they were afraid that one day, I'd show up at the address and bother them or harm them, or secretly break in and steal something. Even if they did give me their address, I couldn't assume that they weren't giving me false information. But for now, I have no choice but to believe that it wasn't false.

"You mean, you remember all seven hundred and fifty of them by their numbers? That's incredible," the woman says.

I feel somewhat pleased, and straighten up my shoulders despite myself. Like the words of an old scholar, who said that giving cultural and historical meaning to a meaningless number creates unexpected drama, the numbers I knew all had a drama of their own. When I say that I remember their drama as well as their number, based on the number alone, the woman's eyes grow wide.

"That's amazing. So why did you give me a number without even asking for my address?" she asks.

"I had to call you by something since you kept following me, and I didn't really want to bother. It doesn't really mean anything," I say.

"When are you going to ask me for my address?"

"I'll see how it goes—I might not even ask at all. 751 is still a temporary number."

That's what I say, but actually, I'm curious as to what kind of a drama will unfold through the number.

"Boy, are you fussy. Are you like that with everyone else, too? Maybe that's why only that many people told you their address," she says.

"What do you mean, only!" I flare up, though I'm not really sure why.

For some reason, I can't seem to speak in a nice way to the woman. It's probably because we didn't meet in such a nice way.

61. Music continues to flow out from the laptop. It's amazing how you can wander around like a nomad and still use the Internet. The term "digital nomad" wasn't coined without reason. Suddenly, the woman begins to tap on the keyboard, mumbling to herself.

"0 believes that numbers don't betray or lie, so why don't they write back?" she says.

I look at her. She stops tapping on the keyboard for a moment, looking as though she's thinking intently on something. Then she begins to mumble again, tilting her head this way and that as though she's talking to someone.

"There could be a number of reasons. Maybe all the addresses were fake; maybe the numbers just didn't want to bother writing; maybe they were illiterate, or indifferent; or maybe they died or moved; maybe they thought the letters were from someone they didn't know, or maybe the letters got lost on their way; maybe they haven't read the letters yet, or didn't like what they said; maybe they're not such great people, or maybe the messenger lied . . ." she goes on.

Listening quietly to her words, I find them all plausible, which suddenly frightens me. I've never considered such possibilities. She must have an extraordinary imagination, since she writes novels. But I'm angry in a way because she has dashed my hopes to the ground. She begins to mumble to herself again.

"Why does he write letters? Does he want to receive letters himself? Or does he write because he's already received them? It's like the question of the chicken or the egg, isn't it?" she asks me, after talking to herself the whole time. I don't answer. Then she begins to talk to herself again.

"I think 0 writes letters because he wants to receive letters. That must be why he says he won't go back home until he gets a reply, right? A letter not sent or delivered is like a letter not written, isn't it? So in the same way, a letter without response is like a letter not written, isn't it?"

"Don't you think you're being too cruel, when you should be comforting me?" I protest.

"All I did was put my imagination to use."

"But you're saying that all the letters I've written up to now have all been in vain."

"Are you mad?"

"How can I not be mad, when you say stuff like that?"

"Your cold is gone, isn't it?"

" . . . ?"

The cold really has left, while I had my mind off it. My body feels as light as cotton. But even if she had really put on the show of wordplay for my sake, my anger doesn't easily subside. I lie down, wrapping the blanket around myself and thinking, tomorrow, I'm going in the opposite direction from her, no matter what.

62. The moonlight shines in through the little motel window. It's the kind of a night when the moonlight would seem much more beautiful with the lights out. The woman is about to turn the lights off, but stops when I tell her that I can't sleep without them. She seems to think that she was doing me a favor by not turning the lights off. But I think since I paid for the room, my habits should be given first priority. I have the bed to myself, and the woman is on the floor with Wajo. She must be having trouble falling asleep because of the light, for she's tossing and turning. She must sense that I'm having trouble falling asleep too, because she initiates a conversation.

"Are you sleeping?"

"How can I sleep, after hearing something like that? It's been three whole years."

"Are you still mad?"

" . . . "

"There will be a number soon who understands how you feel, 0, because numbers are infinite," she says.

" . . . "

I look at the moon. My heart relaxes as the moon shines down on me. As I relax, I feel like asking her questions for no reason.

"Have you ever written a letter?"

"I write e-mails all the time."

"I mean letters on paper, not business e-mails."

"No."

"Never? Have you gotten any, then?"

"No."

"How can you live like that? Don't you get letters from your readers?"

"No."

"Don't you want to?"

"Get letters from readers?"

"Not necessarily letters from readers."

"I do want to get letters, of course."

"If you did, would you write back?"

"Of course I would."

"You don't get any letters because you only think about getting them. If you want to get them, first try sending them. You'll be sure to hear back."

"From looking at you, 0, that doesn't seem to be the case. And who writes letters on paper in this day and age? It's too much hassle. Just finding a mailbox was hard enough. There's a good reason why mailboxes have been disappearing. If you send an e-mail, you might get a reply soon. So next time, ask for their e-mail address, not their home address."

A hassle . . . Still, I don't think all those people would consider it a hassle to write letters on paper. I want to argue.

"They say that people lie more when they write e-mails than when they write letters on paper. I don't like digital correspondence. I like analog letters. You can keep it by your side and take it out and read it whenever and wherever you are. It's inconvenient to have to boot up your computer every time you want to read a letter, and it seems a little cold, and a waste to pay the cost of electricity to read and write a letter. I mean, writing is a basic human act, and to think that it requires money seems a little . . . And a person's character and dignity show through his handwriting, in subtle ways. It can give you vital information about the person. I know that digital methods are great and convenient, but they can't show their true worth without electricity. They're unreliable. Especially for a traveler like me, analog methods suit better," I say.

"But with e-mails, you don't have to pay for writing paper and envelopes and pens. Plus, they're fast and you can check to see if they've been received, and you can cancel the dispatch if you change your mind. In the end, there's a price to be paid either way. We live in a digilog era, when neither the digital nor the analog method alone is enough, so you should use both, combined together. Some people may prefer letters on paper, but some are used to e-mails," she says.

"What matters is the care and thought that can be felt with hands," I say.

"Those things can be found in e-mails, too," she says.

"Let's leave it at that. I don't think talking all night would bring us to an agreement," I say, and roll over toward the window.

The moon shines brightly, and I gently close my eyes.

I ask with my eyes closed, "Aren't you going home? For me the last day of my journey will be the day I get a letter, but when will your journey end, 751?"

I hear her voice come from behind me, saying, "The day I finish my novel."

I open my eyes again.

"You write novels when you travel?"

"Whenever I publish a novel, I go around selling it, and see the world and think about my next novel in the process. When I come up with an idea, I start writing, and when my writing is finished, my journey comes to an end as well," she says.

"So you travel more to write new novels than to sell books? And you get ideas for your novels as you travel around?" I ask.

"Right," she says.

"So in other words, you're an itinerant novelist?"

"To write, it's also important to listen to and observe other people."

"So you followed me because you wanted to observe me?"

"No, because I wanted to hear your story."

"There's more you want to hear?"

"If you have more to tell me, 0."

"How much of your novel have you written?"

"It's almost finished."

"So you'll be going home soon."

"You wish I'd finish it soon, don't you?"

"Of course."

At my cold reply, she shuts her mouth. Have I hurt her feelings?

"Somerset Maugham said that there's no greater exercise of power than to have someone you don't know and haven't met read your works and be moved, and to touch someone's soul and stir up feelings of compassion or fear," I say.

"That's right. Written words are stronger than power. So one day, your letters, 0, will exercise their power and come back to you in the form of a reply," she says.

"You don't need to comfort me," I say.

"I said that because we both write on the road," she says.

I close my eyes again. My cold must be gone, for my body feels light.

63. The first thing I do when I come out of the motel is look for a phone booth. The woman says I'm welcome to use her cell phone, but I politely decline. Traveling becomes relaxing only when you don't rely on digital devices. She puts her rejected phone back in her pocket. The coins drop, and my friend picks up the phone. As soon as he picks up, I begin to hurl words at him in an angry voice. He seems a little flustered.

"What's gotten into you all of a sudden?" he says.

"Have you been lying to me all this time?" I ask.

"About what?"

"Have you been saying that I haven't gotten any letters when I actually have, to screw me over?"

"Would I lie to you when I know what a tough time you're having out on the street? I should get struck by lightning and killed if I did," he says.

In my heart, actually, I'd hoped that he'd been lying. I could put up with a little trick like that, I thought. Which meant that I was growing more and more tired of this journey.

"If you really can't believe me, why don't you come and see for yourself?" he says.

He must've been pretty offended that I doubted him. Today, he's the one who hangs up first.

64. No one wrote me. No doubt, as always.

65. The bus is driving down the highway. As soon as she sits down, the woman turns on her laptop and continues to tap away on the keyboard. She's working on her novel. She looks different from her usual self. She looks calm somehow, and even sexy. Especially when she tucks falling strands of hair behind her ear, or tilts her head and bites down on her lip. I recall what my ex-girlfriend once said, that people look their sexiest not when they've taken off their clothes, but when they're concentrating on their work. The other passengers, however, glare at her as though they're annoyed by the sound of her tapping on the keyboard.

She's the kind of a person who can concentrate on her writing no matter where she is. I know an unhappy person who can't write anything unless he's sitting at his desk in his room with his laptop. He wasn't a novelist, but wanted to be one. He couldn't write while traveling, and even if he did manage to write a little, he'd repeatedly delete and rewrite because he didn't like what he'd written. Even so, the end result wouldn't be to his satisfaction. He said that a piece of writing that wasn't to your satisfaction was useless. What he didn't like probably wasn't what he'd written, but where he was staying. At his request, I read what he wrote. I read things he wrote in his room and things he wrote elsewhere, but I didn't see any difference between them. Actually, what he wrote elsewhere seemed to flow smoother and freer. His unhappiness lay in his notion that his writing varied depending on the place where he wrote, and he didn't even make an attempt to correct the notion.

He soon quit traveling around. No matter what spectacular places he visited, he couldn't enjoy himself because he had only his own room in mind. He was the happiest when he was sitting at his desk in his room, traveling with his laptop. In the end, he became someone who couldn't come out of his room all his life. He did write, of course, but he couldn't be a world-renowned novelist. He could write things that were only as big as the room in which he stayed.

66. The battery must have run out, because the woman closes her laptop. Her face is full of regret that she wasn't able to write more. Frantically, she writes down in a notebook the words she couldn't write on her laptop, as though the sentences may flee or evaporate. From my quiet observation, it looks as though she has a hard time writing on paper. Her handwriting isn't neat, the order is confused, and she often crosses out sentences and squeezes in other sentences in between. It looks as though she's wasting paper.

I look at her and think that most of the people who have gotten my letters may have just as hard a time writing on paper. For a moment, I wonder if I should try writing e-mails. If I sent an e-mail, maybe I'd get a reply, and I'd at least know if the person got my e-mail. Plus I wouldn't have to call and bother my friend, and I wouldn't have to doubt him when he's done so much for me. A reply that arrives as fast as the letter is sent. But the despair, too, would come just as fast. You could click on an e-mail, full of anticipation, only to be deceived by spam. When that occurs to me, I feel that what's slower could be better. Hope that's alive and moving can keep a person going until he falls into despair.

Meanwhile, the bus makes its way into a rest stop. The woman asks me if I'm getting off. I shake my head no. Then she asks me if there's anything I'd like to eat, offering to get it for me. I shake my head again, as if I'm a little annoyed. She puts her belongings down on the seat, asks me to watch them for her, and gets off the bus. Suddenly I have an ominous feeling that she won't be coming back. Why, I wonder. It's probably because of 412.

67. 412, whom I met on an express bus, was someone who sat next to me.

He was friendly, so we quickly became friends. Throughout the bus ride, he told me his life story. He seemed to have led an exciting life. His words came pouring out like those of a medicine peddler, and he was optimistic.

Looking at him, I couldn't help saying, "You've got a great personality. You get that a lot, don't you?"

"Does it seem that way? I wasn't always like this," he said.

"What were you like before?"

"I was fatally cynical, pessimistic, and depressed."

"Oh, come on."

"You don't believe me, do you? I never imagined myself that I'd change so much."

412 said that it was a high school friend who made him so talkative and cheerful. When I thought about it, the friend was always in the story when he was talking excitedly about his life. By then, I was more fascinated by the friend than by 412, and our conversation naturally turned toward the friend. At the end of our conversation, he said that he was on his way to meet his friend. Then the following words popped out of my mouth.

"Could I meet him, too?"

I probably said that because I, too, wanted to be infected by the positive virus from his friend. Immediately, I clapped my hands over my mouth, as though I'd made a big mistake, but he was neither flustered nor surprised. He said that whenever he told people about his friend, they all begged him to let them meet him.

"You'll probably fall for him as soon as you see him, too," he said.

What does someone who makes you fall for him as soon as you see him look like? I wondered. 412 looked a little sad, however, after saying those words. Having gotten his consent more easily than I'd expected, I changed my destination on the moving bus. I was very excited at the prospect of meeting his friend, and asked him for his address while I was at it. As I entered the address into my mind, the bus entered the rest stop. 412 told me that he was getting a cup of coffee, asked me to watch his stuff for him, and got off the bus.

412, however, never came back on the bus. I pled with the driver to wait a little more because there was someone who wasn't back, but the driver had other passengers to consider. Thanks to the driver, I was able to wait five more minutes, but 412 never came back. In the end, the bus made its departure, and I stood on the entrance steps looking in the direction of the rest stop until the bus entered the highway. 412 was nowhere to be seen. I came back and sat down on my seat. I saw the stuff 412 had asked me to watch. It was a good thing, I thought, that he hadn't asked me to watch a newborn baby or a puppy. I got off at my original destination with his stuff in hand. The next morning, I sent a letter, along with his stuff, asking why he never came back on the bus.

68. Suddenly I feel anxious that the woman, like 412, may not return. Should I have asked her for a bottle of water or something? I leap to my feet and look out the window, which isn't like me. Even if she doesn't come back, I can't send her stuff in the mail as I did for 412. Should I have asked for her address earlier? I can easily get it by calling her publisher, I think, and flop back down on my seat. It also occurs to me that I'm a little silly for thinking such thoughts. Just yesterday, I was wishing that we could go our separate ways, that she would finish writing her novel soon. Trying to relax, I cross my arms and close my eyes. At that moment, the bus lurches to a start.

My eyes fly open, and I jump from my seat like a spring puppet and shout out to the driver, "There's someone missing!"

The driver turns his head and looks at me. I make my way toward the entrance and look out the window as I did earlier. A few restless seconds go by. The driver frowns. The bus lurches a little backwards. I grow more restless and take a step onto the entrance steps. A few more seconds pass. The bus is approaching the road. At that moment, I see the woman in the distance, running toward the bus. She's running as fast as she can, looking ridiculous. So ridiculous that it almost makes me laugh. But I suppress my laughter and turn right around, and sit back down on my seat. The woman, out of breath, keeps bowing to the driver in apology, and sits down on her seat.

"You could've missed the bus! Where were you?" I say to her, as though scolding a child.

Still out of breath, she replies, "I, have no sense, of direction, so it took, a little while, to find the bus."

"I wouldn't say a little!"

"Were you worried? That I, might have run away, after asking you, to watch my baggage?"

Instead of answering her, I turn my head toward the window like a sulking child. She brings up to Wajo's nose the fishcakes and dumplings she bought at the rest stop. Wajo sniffs and wolfs them down. She taps me on the arm and offers me some. I take a look, and turn my head back toward the window.

"This baggage is my life. Would I abandon it and run?" she says.

"Some people do."

"Would you abandon Wajo and run, 0?"

"That's different."

"It's the same to me."

I look at Wajo, absorbed in eating. Is Wajo my life, or my baggage? In a way, he's the one who has led me to this point, so he must be my life. If I had considered him baggage, I would've come without him in the first place. I turn my head toward the window. The bus is picking up speed on the highway, and the woman resumes writing her novel in a little notebook.

69. As soon as she gets off the bus, the woman stands in the middle of the terminal square and begins selling books as if in a performance. Without my help now, she gives a reading, introduces herself, answers the audience's questions, signs the books, and takes pictures, standing side by side with the audience and holding up the books she has signed. In this way, the books get sold off one by one. The people show more interest in the woman, who's selling her own novels, than in her books. She carries out the task, which some writers may consider humiliating, as though it were her calling in life. I sit on the clock tower far away from her and look at her as though she were a stranger. There's a faint smile hanging at the corner of her lips. The weather is the hottest it's been this summer.

As the people scatter away one by one, the woman comes over to the clock tower, pulling her cart. I put *The Moon and Sixpence*, which I'd been holding in my hand, into my backpack. Lately, I've been feeling lonelier while reading. I think it's because I read novels, and novels are about people. If there's a novel with only one character, it wouldn't make me feel lonely. When I think about it, I don't think I've ever read a novel with only one character. A novel like that probably doesn't even exist.

When I've finished speaking, the woman says, "Well, then, don't read them."

"I figure I'll look less lonely with a book in my hand."

"So you're the type that cares what other people think."

"That's how you end up when you go around alone. People think people who go around alone are weird."

"I know what you mean. I often care what people think, too. But in the end, everyone is alone in the world."

"Everyone is alone, but not everyone thinks so."

"You have Wajo."

"People don't consider Wajo a person."

"If you're not lonely because you have Wajo, that means you're not alone. Wajo would be disappointed if he heard what you just said. It's arrogant to think that only people can heal loneliness."

"Have you ever read a novel with only one character?"

She furrows her brows, looking intent.

"No," she answers.

"That's because there's no such novel. There's no such novel, because people can't do anything alone. Do you think such a novel exists somewhere I don't know about?"

"Well, if there isn't, I'll write one myself."

"Even if you did, it'd be a very tedious and boring novel."

"You never know."

She starts taking pictures with great enthusiasm, as though clicking the camera shutter is the same thing as writing a novel. When she points the camera at me, I let out a yelp and cover my face with my arms. I hate pictures more than anything in the world. Pictures are tragic things that turn into pain, sorrow, and anguish in the end. I don't know why people are so desperate to capture tragedy, why they struggle to get at least one picture. People mistake the flash that explodes every time a picture is taken for a blessing. The light is not a blessing, but a splendid method of disguise to cover up the tragedy called a picture. Darkness begins where light ends.

"Why do you take pictures, when you can just remember?" I ask.

"Someone with a good memory like you, 0, may not need them, but someone with a bad memory like me does."

"Why?"

"Because novels consist of descriptions and reenactments."

"So you take pictures for your novels?"

"If I could reduce things to numbers, too, I wouldn't need something as cumbersome as this."

Am I blessed, indeed? Free of encumbrance? How simple and easy, then. And how liberated I am. Because I can live without the blessing of light, my memory becomes more rich and fertile, and other people's lives won't become tragic because of me. Real tragedy is not my own, experienced by me, but other people's tragedy experienced because of me.

The woman no longer points the camera at me.

70. News flows out from an electronics dealership, saying that the temperature has hit a record high. The woman seems exhausted, and Wajo flops down on the ground as though in protest, his tongue hanging out. I pull his leash, but he doesn't budge. I find a bit of shadow and duck into it, but the shadow, too, has long been encroached upon by the sultry weather. It seems that we'll all collapse from sunstroke. The woman, pleading dizziness, suggests that we go in somewhere. We make our way toward the nearest motel from where we're standing.

Motels are secretive, and almost always suggestive.

No matter how much I insist that I'm just there for a "rest," no one would believe me now. The woman and I are a couple in anyone's eyes, and a couple who goes in and out of motel rooms in the middle of the day, at that. The receptionist asks without reserve, "Here for a rest, right?" in a conclusive way, as though there are only so many things that a couple, who crawls into a motel room in the middle of the day, can do there. The look on his face seems to say, what good will it do to roll around on such a stifling day? The place is called Motel Banana, to boot. I tell the receptionist who's handing me the room key that we're staying the night, and he looks at me as if in awe. But I put up with him because he generously lets Wajo in.

The woman suggests that since we're sharing a room, we should use the money saved to get some food that will help regain strength. I say yes without a thought because it's so hot. It doesn't feel at all awkward as we enter the motel room side by side, probably because it's not the first time we're sharing a room. Exhausted from the heat, we collapse and fall asleep as soon as we enter the room. I don't know where the time flies.

71. I open my eyes. The room is dark. The woman and Wajo are taking turns snoring rhythmically. It's dark out the window, too. An unbearably sour stench rises up from every part of my body. The room, too, is reeking of sweat. I get up from my bed and go into the bathroom to take a shower. I can't help feeling uncomfortable with the woman in the room. I'm in the habit of going around naked in motel rooms, but I can't do that now. I must put on the underwear I just washed, and I can't even wash my clothes, which are drenched in sweat. I wash my hair and put the clothes back on. When I do, the sweaty odor seems to seep back into my body. I can't keep them on, I'm so uncomfortable. They render the shower meaningless, and dispel the refreshing memory. I take the clothes back off, put them in the sink, and rub them clean. A luxury motel would be equipped with robes, but there's none here. I come out only in my underwear and wrap myself in a blanket.

72. The woman and Wajo wake up at simultaneously an hour later. She just washes her hair without taking a shower. It seems that she just carelessly wiped her body using a wet towel before changing into new clothes and coming out of the bathroom. At first I think it's because she's embarrassed to have me hear her taking a shower, but that's not it.

"I'm going to sweat a bucket again tomorrow anyway, so why should I take a shower?" she says.

"It wouldn't matter if you were by yourself, but you should give the person next to you some thought."

She sniffs herself and says, "So what if I smell a little? It's not like we're clinging to each other."

She doesn't wash very often, and is kind of dirty. She doesn't care what people think, either. In any case, she's very odd. People who write must generally be that way. The unfortunate man who couldn't write unless he was in his own room disliked washing as much as the woman. He wouldn't take a shower until he finished writing, and wouldn't wash his hair or cut his fingernails, either. I could guess how far his work had progressed by the length of his fingernails. He later formed the habit of collecting his fingernails. When he showed me a glass jar full of fingernails in the shape of crescent moons, collected over a period of ten years, the first thought that came to my mind was that it was a good thing that they were fingernails, since fingernails are small and white, at least. It would've been too awful if they had been hair, bulky and black.

The woman takes poor, innocent Wajo into the bathroom. She lathers up soap and washes every part of him as if she can't forgive his smell, even though she gives no heed to her own body odor. Wajo must feel refreshed, for he falls back into sleep after his bath. The warmest, most restful sleep in the world washes over you after a shower.

73. Three bowls of *samgyetang* ordered with the money saved on the room, are delivered to the room. Wajo, who's been sleeping, gets to his feet and follows the smell to the bowls. The woman and I bone some chicken for Wajo, and take a drumstick each and begin to scarf it down like savages. It was a good idea to save on the room. *Samgyetang* is the best way to boost your health in the middle of the summer.

I'm digging into the tough breast meat when I hear a loud noise from outside. We look at each other with greasy faces and strain our ears. Someone out there is kicking a door. This happens sometimes when you're staying at a motel. You can get a general idea of what's going on even without looking. The couple staying in the room is probably having an affair, and the person outside kicking the door is probably married to one of them. The person outside has grasped the outrageous fact that his or her spouse is having an affair, and has come to raid the scene of the crime. I hear the voice of the person in question. "Open the door! I know everything!" It's a deep male voice. The situation becomes more clear and complex. The man has come to catch his wife in the act. When I say that, the woman devours a chicken wing in a single bite, sucks noisily on the bone, and shakes her head no.

"What are you saying?" I ask.

"You never know until you see it with your own eyes."

"Want to make a bet?"

"What kind of a bet?"

"If I'm wrong, you can have the bed tonight."

"All right."

Finally, we hear the door opening from the inside. We go right up to our door, and put our ears against it. We hear the sound of people hitting each other, and the sound of someone screaming. Soon the man will be walking out of the motel, dragging his half-naked wife by the wrist. We open the door quietly and peek outside. It's the room at the end of the corridor.

At last, the people in question are about to reveal themselves. Just as I predicted, a man is pulling someone out by a thin wrist. The person inside seems to be struggling not to go outside. But to no avail. The person comes flying out of the room by the man's force. Then the other person comes out, clutching a gray suit. Wrapped in a blanket, I stare through the crack in the door at the people walking through the corridor. My mouth hangs open. All three are men, solidly built.

I close the door, turn around, and ask the woman, "How did you know?"

"Just by the tremor in their voices," she says.

"What's the difference?" I ask, mystified.

"I can't really explain; it's just a feeling I get," she says nonchalantly.

She finishes off the chicken soup and lies down on the bed. Suddenly, I'm afraid that she might have caught on. That by the tremor in my voice, she might have become aware of how I feel. That more and more, I'm enjoying being with her. That more and more, I'm growing comfortable with, and used to, being with another person.

74. From the adjacent room comes the sound of a woman moaning. An awkward feeling hovers between the woman and me. At times like this, I wonder why the act of love was created to be accompanied by noise. Couldn't the human body have been made more pliable, so that the intimate act could be undertaken in silence? I feel as if the creaking noise is causing cracks between us. I wish I could go next door and oil up the couple's bodies. I'm well aware, of course, that there's no pleasure without pain. Perhaps it's noise that allows pain to turn into pleasure, and pleasure into pain.

The moaning next door does not cease even after twenty minutes. The woman, probably embarrassed, strikes up a conversation. Hoping that our voices will muffle the noise from beyond the wall.

"What did you pack in your backpack when you left home?" she asks.

The question seems to have been improvised so that we may escape the awkward moment.

"Why do you care what other people carry in their backpacks?" I ask in return.

"Because they must have packed what they need the most, which must be their most necessary desire."

"An MP3 player and a novel."

"Those things are poles apart."

"What about you, 751?"

"A harmonica and a laptop."

"Music and words. We're not all that different."

The woman next door must have reached orgasm, because the moaning suddenly escalates. It's so loud that this time, I improvise a question, hoping it'll lead our excited nerves elsewhere.

"Why a harmonica?"

"Because it's small and cheap, and can express the notes clearly."

The question fades away, and silence falls. Again, we're embarrassed. The woman, unable to endure the silence, starts to rattle on as though in a soliloquy.

"I had a little sister. She loved music and was a talented composer. Unfortunately, she got into a car accident when she was in elementary school and had to have her left arm amputated. Almost all the refined instruments in the world require ten fingers. The piano, the flute, the guitar, the violin, and even the recorder. There are, of course, countless things in the world you can do with only one arm. You can write, you can drive, you can shake hands. You can have sex, too, of course. But my sister thought that she couldn't perform music. The harmonica was the instrument I recommended to my sister, who was in despair. Because the harmonica is an instrument you play with your mouth, not your hands. You can play it with only one arm, or with no arm at all, even. My sister thought it would be meaningless if she couldn't play firsthand the songs she had written. So she played the harmonica fervently. She probably couldn't help it. When she picked up the harmonica, I played along with her. What's really sad is that she could never give up the piano, with its refined sound. Later, she asked me to learn how to play the piano for her. And to play the songs she wrote. I told her no. She couldn't understand me, who played only the harmonica when I had two arms. She probably hated me."

"Why didn't you just learn how to play? It's not that difficult."

"I wanted to show her that there were people who could play only the harmonica even when they had two arms. If I played the piano with my two healthy arms, she would've fallen into even deeper despair."

"Does she still play the harmonica?"

"She died."

"How . . . ?"

"A harmonica is just a harmonica; it can't be a piano. I think it's a good thing she died. Living like that is a tragedy."

"I want to hear the songs she wrote."

"All the songs I played on the harmonica are hers."

"Don't you play any other songs on the harmonica?"

"No."

"Why not?"

"Because my sister's songs are the only songs I can play on the harmonica, and the harmonica is the only instrument with which her songs can be played."

While I was listening attentively to her story, the moaning next door came to an end. A calm, comfortable silence remained between us for quite some time. The stillness continued, and it seemed now that it shouldn't be broken by anyone. Suddenly, I wanted to write a letter. I took out some paper and a pencil from my backpack and lay face down on the floor. The woman took out her harmonica and began to play her sister's songs, looking up at the ceiling. She held the harmonica with only her right hand. Now that I think about it, it seems that she's always played the harmonica with just one hand.

75. I write, listening to her playing the harmonica.

Dear Older Brother,

What kind of a little brother was I? The question occurred
to me as I listened to someone talk about her little sister
today. I don't think I've ever asked a question like that
before, either to myself or to you. If I asked you now,
would you answer? I probably don't even need to ask,
because you'd probably say, "Hey, buster, you were a little
brat who always went around embarrassing me. Can't
you do something about your stuttering? If you did just
that, I'll accept you as my little brother." Since I no longer
stutter, I'm sure you'll approve, as far as that matter goes.
If so, it'll be the first time you ever approve of me.

I wonder if, perhaps, you aren't more curious than I
am. As to what kind of a brother you were to me. You
probably haven't ever asked that question, either, to
yourself or to me. But you probably don't need to ask.
Because you were always someone I approved of. And
because you already knew that you were my idol, my
pride. You were perfection itself. You never allowed for
a single weak spot in you, not enough room for even a
needle to penetrate, to the point of frustration. I know, of
course, why you had to be so perfect. I know that you had
no choice but to live like that, because of me, an idiot who
always came home beaten up. I know you had no choice
but to give up all the fun in the world and do enough
studying for both of us so that you could be a good son to
Mother and Father, who were unhappy about me. I really
must've been an idiot, because back then, I thought you
liked studying and had fun doing it. I assumed that you
were a dull person who wrote down "studying" as your
hobby or specialty. I learned through Eunyeong that you
hated studying as much as I did. You remember her, don't

you? The girl who was always in charge of the exposition during student mass because she had a good voice.

Eunyeong was your first love, but she was mine, too. And the first person ever to make you, as well as me, despair. I envied you so much because everyone showered you with attention. As my envy turned into monstrous jealousy, I wanted to defeat you just once before I died. By then I was used to being known as so-and-so's brother at school or church, which made me want to beat you even more. It was too late to beat you academically, so I had to get busy looking for something else. No matter how perfect you were, I thought, there had to be a weak spot in you. That's when I noticed Eunyeong. Or I should say, the way you looked at Eunyeong. You were in love. That's when I realized for the first time that you, too, were a human being with a heart that could love someone. The weak spot, the target of attack, was determined: your heart.

You went to church not to meet Jesus, but Eunyeong, and at last, opportunity came your way. With Christmas a week away, we had to put up a tree. We hung light bulbs and decorations at random on a fir tree, and in the box was the last piece: the gold star for the top. We were all waiting for someone else to do the job, because the tree was too tall and we lacked courage. Then bravely, Eunyeong took the star and went up to the ladder. You stopped her by the arm, as if according to a TV script. Following the script, you climbed up the ladder to the ceiling and hung the star at the top despite your fear of heights. Solely for Eunyeong. I saw her eyes, looking at you, sparkle like that star. You and Eunyeong hid behind the tree on Christmas Eve and shared a very deep kiss. The kiss was a signal to me. A signal to approach Eunyeong.

I met Eunyeong often without your knowledge. It was when you were studying, enduring pains to be number one nationwide. So those moments became even sweeter for me. Eunyeong opened up to me more easily than I'd expected. Later, she even told me that you, such a good student, were a bit overwhelming for her. She also said that she wished you were ordinary like me. For the first time since I was born, I didn't envy you, and was happy that I was myself. It was while painting Easter eggs that I won her over completely. That day, her breasts were as small as the eggs. Thinking of you, I held the eggs for a long time against my own breast.

I think that was when you missed the top ranking for the first time. Your heart broke down as well. I really couldn't believe it. That your heart could break down over something so trivial as love. Only when I saw you go into the operating room did I realize what I'd done. You were the unhappiest person I knew. Someone who couldn't love, someone who couldn't do anything other than be number one, someone who had to be number one even though he didn't want to. You didn't love anyone after that. It wasn't that you hated me, though. You used the time that could have been used to love or hate someone to study more. You were the real idiot. Not me.

It was around that time that I stopped going to the public bath with you. I couldn't bring myself to look at the scar on your chest. It was around that time, too, that I came to really like you and trust you. I often did as you did because I wanted your approval, believed every word you said, and did everything you told me to. I couldn't go wrong when I was doing what you told me to do. It was quicker to ask for your opinion than to sit at church praying to Jesus. When Mother decided what my job would be, I wouldn't have had the guts to go with it if you hadn't been at my side, giving me advice. Just as you said, the job was right for me. Maybe I worked harder because I wanted you to be right. You were the person who had the most influence on my life. That night, you held my hand tight and said, "Do what you want with your life." It was what you said to me on the train when we ran away from home. You know that those words played a part in my decision to come on this difficult journey, don't you? Thank you. For letting me do what I want with my life. Without you, I wouldn't have found this overflowing freedom, or enjoyed it.

Now it's my turn. My turn to save you. I don't know if it'll work, but put your trust in me. It's not too late yet. There's a chance for you to do what you want with your life. Like we did back then, you can just run and get on a train, and clap your hands when you see a tunnel. And when you come out through the long tunnel, you'll have changed for sure. Like I did.

I want to end this journey soon, if only to get on a train with you. See you soon. Till then, take care.

Your little brother, from Motel Banana

76. The woman, who went to get some air because she was having trouble falling asleep, comes back with four cans of beer and two bags of squid and peanut flavored snack.

She opens a can and hands it to me, saying, "How about a movie?"

"You want to go to the movies at this hour?"

"Who would go to the movies at this hour?"

She takes out her laptop from her backpack and asks me if there's anything I'd like to see.

The word "movie" strikes me as unfamiliar. I never went to the movies on my journey. I rarely watched TV, either. Perhaps I thought that a journey began only when you broke free from the habits of civilized people, or city people. How would a journey, undertaken with such trouble, be any different from ordinary life? And if it wasn't different, it'd be meaningless, I thought. Above all, if there was no difference between a journey and everyday life, I wouldn't feel that I had come on a journey.

"It's been so long since I saw a movie that I don't even know what's out," I say.

"Then just watch what I recommend," she says.

It seems that she's often watched a movie even while traveling. She goes onto a movie download site and begins a search.

"Are you doing an illegal download?" I ask.

"Don't worry. I paid for it. It's going to take a while, because the wireless signal is weak," she says.

She frets, watching the download bar that's moving too slowly. I've thought this before, but she doesn't seem to have a knack for waiting patiently.

"Just wait. They're telling you kindly that there are forty more minutes to go," I say.

"Should we try moving the laptop near the door?"

"How do you write, when you're so impatient?"

"Write? I don't know. It's strange how mellow I get when I write. All the men in the world would fall in love with me if they saw me working on a novel."

"Where does that unfounded confidence come from?"

Despite my words, I recall the way she'd looked, tapping away on her laptop on the bus. I'd found her quite sexy.

"So why are you still alone?" I ask.

"Because you usually write novels when you're alone. It's

something you don't get to see easily, or show, for that matter," she says.

"Show me."

"I can't, because when I know that someone's watching, I turn into my usual self. And I can't write very well, either."

"So you need to meet a man who likes the way you look when you're not writing a novel, huh?"

"There's never been a man like that."

"That doesn't surprise me."

"What?"

"What if there was one?"

"Even if there was, I wouldn't want him!"

"Why not? Do you plan on staying single?"

"I can't do anything that involves two or more people. I can't, because it's too difficult to keep the rhythm or beat. That's why I've never had sex, or been married."

There are people in the world who are unhappy because they have no one to keep the rhythm or beat with, even if they want to. Is she happy, compared to such people?

"You've never tried it?"

"What? Marriage? Sex?"

"Sex."

"Of course I have. I made an effort, but something was off and we both felt awkward, so I didn't really try after that . . ."

She shakes her head from side to side as though she doesn't want to remember, and shrugs her shoulders.

"Marriage is one thing, but how can you write novels when you don't understand sex?" I ask.

"A novel doesn't equal sex," she replies.

"I guess you're right."

"I don't play badminton, either. People think it's strange when you're alone in doing something that's usually done by two people. Watching a movie or eating, for instance. Like there's a rule that such things should be done by two or more people. That's why I like doing things that don't seem strange at all even when you're doing them alone."

"Such as?"

"Going to the beauty salon, jumping ropes, things like that. Well, of course, it's just as strange to do something with another person that should be done alone."

"Like?"

"Reading or playing the harmonica."

"Is that why you became a novelist?"

"I wrote screenplays at first. Once, I stayed cooped up in a little room for days with a close friend of mine, writing a screenplay. We were doing fine, until a little problem occurred. There was a difference in opinions, with my friend saying that the next line should be 'That's not possible,' and me saying that it should be 'No.' In a way, it was only a little line that couldn't possibly have a critical impact on the quality of the work, because no one would know the difference."

"So what happened?"

"Neither of us backed off a single step. Each insisted that her own line be used. In the end, we both became extremely upset. Furious, I dealt her the first blow. Her nose bled, and she pulled out a fistful of my hair. That's when I began to dislike doing things with another person, because I was sick and tired of it. The idea of two stirs up a strange feeling in me. Not a very good feeling."

"You could write a screenplay on your own, couldn't you?"

"I couldn't anymore, because writing a screenplay is a task that always leaves the possibility of two people working together. The idea kept making me nervous."

"But writing novels doesn't make you nervous?"

"No."

"It makes you lonely, though."

"I don't really know what it's like to be lonely, because I haven't been with another person very often."

"Is it strange to be with me, then?"

"We're not doing anything together. We're just with each other."

"We're drinking together. We're going to be watching a movie together in a bit, and we've been together this whole time, haven't we?"

"I guess you're right."

She rolls her eyes, taking a gulp of her beer.

"What I do know for sure is that it doesn't feel the way it did when I was with someone in the past."

"How does it feel, then?"

"I just feel like I'm alone."

Disappointed, I gulp down my beer. We still have to wait twenty more minutes for the download to be complete.

77. "How long have you wanted to be a writer?" I ask.

The woman takes careful bites of the shells surrounding the peanuts, and collects the peanuts in the palm of her hand. When she has collected a number of peanuts, she takes a sip of her beer and pops them into her mouth all at once.

"My father owned a print shop," she says.

Again, she begins to collect the peanuts in the palm of her hand.

"So I grew up breathing in the smell of paper and ink. People didn't like the smell, saying it gave them a headache, but I really liked it. From time to time, these people, these writers, came to the shop. To see how their books came out, you know. They watched their words being printed on paper, with a look of satisfaction and wonder on their faces. To my father, they must have seemed the happiest people in the world. One day, sitting with his chin in his hand in a corner of the shop and staring at the machine at work, he said, 'I hope my daughter becomes a happy person, too ...'" she says.

Again, she pops the peanuts in her palm into her mouth all at once and crunches on them.

"My father must've been bored one day, because when the machines in the shop were at rest, he collected all the things I'd written and turned them into a book. It was pretty decent, with a title on the cover and even a profile photo. No, it wasn't just pretty decent; it was a real book. I took it, with a mysterious feeling in my heart. The numbers on the pages looked like latitudes and longitudes on a map, or like street numbers, like they wouldn't go anywhere. The sentences, neatly printed on paper, looked elegant and profound, and every sentence smelled of ink. That's when I first thought, books are quite wonderful," she says.

She must have grown tired of separating the peanuts from the snack, for she just puts it in her mouth and munches on it.

"But later, I became a little depressed that I was the only one who had and knew about the book. More and more, I wanted to write a book that a lot of people would know about and keep in their possession. Now I understand the value of such. Things went the way my father had hoped and planned for."

"Your father must've been very happy that you became a writer."

"He passed away before he got to see me as a writer. My oldest brother is in charge of the print shop now."

"Are you happy?"

"I should be, if only for my father."

78. My father often said such things, too, sitting in a corner of his shop. That he wished he had a child who would take charge of the shop for him. My father, who quit his job as a physics teacher to become an inventor, opened a toy shop that same year.

He had my mother to consider, and invention wasn't something that would bring in money right away, so he needed something that would bring in a regular income. In addition, owning a toy shop was a dream he'd had since he was a child. Now that I think about it, my father, more than anyone else, was someone who did what he wanted with his life, without caring what other people thought.

My father was more suited to be a toy-shop owner than an inventor. He himself wanted to be known more as a toy-shop owner than an inventor, and in his old age, he wanted to remain a toy-shop owner. My mother, of course, wasn't happy that he had become someone who sold toys. I think she looked down on him a little, too, because what he was doing seemed undignified for someone of his age and social position, like a game played by immature children. Whenever my mother heaved a sigh, my father urged her not to look down on toys. Fortunately, her discontent didn't last long, because the business thrived and the toys made a solid contribution to the household income.

The three of us—my brother, my sister, and I—often played in the toy shop. My brother usually played with robots, I liked cars and airplanes, and Jiyun, ever the girl that she was, became absorbed in changing doll clothes.

One day, my father asked, looking down at the top of our heads, "Will any of you take charge of this shop for me?"

No one paid attention to his words, because we were engrossed in playing with the toys. Then my father spoke again, in a more earnest voice, saying, "A long time from now, I mean."

I looked over at my brother and Jiyun. It was obvious to anyone that my brother was more fit for academics than business, and Jiyun didn't have the patience to spend her life cooped up in a tiny shop. It was obvious that she thought running a business was a boring job that ate away at her time. Then my father's eyes met mine. I knew. I knew that from the beginning, he'd had me in mind when he spoke those words. I bent my head down toward the toys, avoiding his eyes.

Ten years later, when I was in college, my father said, "Your mother looked down on those toys, but they're not something to be taken lightly."

My father believed that a great life began with games. Just as his dream of becoming an inventor began with a trivial game, the future could begin with a game, he said. He thought that a toy on display at the shop could change someone's destiny, like a game. When I heard that, I thought, a toy shop may be the greatest shop in the world. I answered the question my father had asked ten years before. In other words, I'd needed ten years to give that answer.

"Don't worry. A long time from now, I'll take charge of the shop for you," I said.

My father seemed to feel that his remaining days would no longer be uncertain. And at the same time, the feelings of discomfort that had tormented me for ten years vanished without a trace from my heart.

79. When I finish speaking, the woman says, "That makes me want to learn more about toy shops, somehow."

When I empty a can of beer, she offers another. I don't decline.

"When do you plan to take over the shop?" she asks.

"I don't know for sure, but it could be the day I end my journey and return home . . . There's not much else for me to do, anyway."

"What did you do before?"

"I was a government employee."

"That must've been a boring job."

"Not as boring as you'd think. It kept me quite busy."

"All the government employees I knew always looked like they were so bored, they could die. It seemed that they had a lot of time on their hands, sitting at their desks and doing their nails or chatting online. They do nothing but sponge off tax money."

"I wasn't a desk employee, so I didn't have the time to do my nails."

"What kind of an employee were you, then?"

I take a gulp of my beer and say with a chuckle, "I was in technical post. A postman."

She looks at me, a little surprised, and asks, "You were a postman?"

"Is that so surprising?"

"No, just a little unexpected."

80. To be honest, it had been a little unexpected for me as well. I had never imagined that I'd become a postman. There probably aren't that many people who imagine that their future job will be that of a postman. Most people imagine themselves as a doctor, a judge, or an astronaut—not a postman. I was the same.

It was my mother who bestowed upon me the job of a postman. My mother was always on edge because of me. My brother and Jiyun knew where they were headed so they didn't present a problem, but I was different. For my mother, I was a child she had to take care of in every little way, because I was somewhat slow and insecure, and sickly as well.

It seems that in my mother's eyes, I was someone who couldn't even get a decent job. Until I graduated from college, my mother worried endlessly about my future job. Because she did all my worrying for me, so much so that it showed, I ended up entrusting my future into her hands. I was a problem child, even in my own opinion. In my mind, of course, a countless number of jobs I wanted danced around and around. On days with continuing newsflashes because of a big accident, such as an airplane crash, I wanted to be an announcer; when looking at the big chalkboard hanging in my mother's study, I wanted to be a teacher; on days with a clear sky, I wanted to be a journalist; when the wind blew, I wanted to be a stage actor. But I could not talk to anyone about these jobs. No one would think such jobs were possible for me. Desire had a wicked habit of not knowing its place, and trying to go beyond that. Most of the jobs I wanted would be impossible for someone who stuttered.

One day, my mother called out my name in a tense voice, probably with a headache from worrying for too long over a problem that had no answer. "What are we going to do with you? Do you hear me? Come here, Jihun! What are you going to be? Come here, I said, you idiot! If there's anything you want to be, why don't you tell me, at least? Jihun! Jihun!" It seemed that she would go on nagging till the next morning. I locked the bathroom door and sat on the toilet, my ears covered up. I could still hear her shrill voice even with my ears covered up, so I began to sing.

By the time I'd sung about ten songs, my mother's nagging had come to a stop. The silence, it seemed, would soon make my breathing come to a stop as well. I pushed the toilet lever and came out of the bathroom. My mother was sitting on the living room sofa, waiting for me. Everyone else was sitting on the sofa as well, looking grave. My mother gestured busily at me, telling me to hurry. Like a slug, I slowly made my way over to an empty seat and sat down, as though I didn't care at all about how urgent she felt.

"Deliver letters," my mother said abruptly.

She went on, saying, "Have you ever talked to the postman?"

"N-no," I said.

"Me neither. None of us have. All they have to do is deliver letters promptly. Words aren't necessary as long as they do their job, and they don't need to talk much. You wouldn't feel uncomfortable or nervous, either, since you won't be coming into direct contact with people very often," she said.

I raised my head and looked around at my family. Everyone seemed to agree with what my mother was saying.

"One of your father's friends is a postmaster. He'll write you a recommendation, if your father requests. I'm not saying that you need to become a postman right away. You can work part time during summer break. Then if you find that it doesn't suit you or is too difficult, you can quit," she said.

I already knew then that I couldn't quit, even if it didn't suit me or was too difficult; that if I ever did quit, my mother would be greatly disappointed in me.

When she finished speaking, my brother contributed, saying in a calm voice, "You'll be bringing people news."

His words seemed to encourage me a little. A job that allows you to bring people news. That could be worthwhile, I thought.

81. Following my brother's advice that they'd be required for postal service, I obtained a driver's license, a motorcycle license, and a computer certification before the break began. The licenses were very easy to obtain, since they didn't require speaking. I started out as a delivery assistant with the recommendation of my father's friend. My father had asserted to his friend that I'd be excellent in memorizing the delivery routes because I had an exceptional memory. He was right. The person who was teaching me how to do the job was so surprised that he nearly fainted. Usually, they followed you around for a week teaching you how to do the job, but I memorized the delivery routes all in a day. He stared at me, looking dazed, and said, "I've never seen anyone like you. You have a gift for making deliveries." In that moment, I felt, for the first time, that nothing brings you so much joy in

life as being approved of by someone. Out of a desire for further approval and praise, I worked even harder to become familiar with the task of delivering letters. My only problem was that I was out of shape, but since the job required a lot of moving around, I gradually became more fit.

After successfully passing through what were supposed to be the two most difficult months on the job, I kept at it even after graduation. It somehow worked out that way. There were things about the job that suited my disposition, but more than that, the thought of going in search of a new job made me feel hopeless, and the thought of making my body adjust to that new job made me feel even more hopeless. Some postmen said that they'd rather recommend being a street cleaner because being a postman meant low pay and hard work, but I was of the opinion that something so trivial as physical fatigue should be endured. Thus I endured, working for a year on fatigue duty, and six more months as a contract worker. I became qualified for an exam relatively soon, and applied for and passed the regular exam held by the Post Office in order to become an official postman. At last, I was an official government employee, not just a temporary worker.

It was my mother, of course, who rejoiced the most at the news of my success. She was proud that she had found me a job through which I could earn my living. She was pleased beyond measure that the job was that of a government employee, no less. They may say that a certain job brings in a lot of money, or looks respectable, but parents are bound to consider best a job that draws a government stipend. As I entered the stable world of government employees, my mother treated me in a stable way, and lived her life with a stable heart. When my problem was resolved, my mother looked at peace, like someone who no longer had any worries.

82. As for me, however, most of the days weren't so peaceful. My belief that something as trivial as physical fatigue should be endured was beginning to deteriorate. They say that the development of e-mail has led to a reduction in the quantity of mail, but still, there was a mountain of work to be done. Contrary to what it seems, even just putting mail in the mailbox wasn't an easy task, and my palms got chapped, and sometimes, my fingernails even fell out. On days when there was snow or rain, not to mention heat waves or bitter cold, I had to be on my guard so that the mail wouldn't get wet. Sometimes, I got into accidents with my motorcycle, skidding on the slippery ground. Even if I got done with the mail delivery early, I had to go back to the post office and work on sorting out the mail. Getting off work on time was a rare event that occurred only a few times a year, and on holidays or during election seasons, I had to work past eleven o'clock at night. It wasn't easy to get the weekends off, either. The biggest problem, though, was dealing with customers. My family had said that they'd never talked to a postman or struck up a conversation with one, but that was just in my family's case. Immature kids called me "postie," and customers often struck up conversations with me. In some cases, I couldn't help getting into a scuffle, with customers talking down to me or picking a fight. When I was handling registered mail, in particular, I couldn't help but talk to the recipients because I had to deliver the mail directly to them. I'd break out in a cold sweat and stutter in front of them, of course, and they'd get frustrated, and then annoyed. The only thing I could do to minimize conflict with customers was not to make a mistake in delivery.

But I couldn't complain to my family about all the difficulties. I couldn't, and didn't, let on that I was having a hard time. There were bound to be difficulties in any job, I thought, and there probably wasn't any easy way in the world to make money. Above all, I no longer wanted to be a disappointment to someone, and I was old enough that I shouldn't be a disappointment. So I didn't say anything to my family, acting as if the job were my calling in life, and after a long time, when I was efficient at my job, I did come to think of it as my calling in life. But I grew more and more quiet and reticent at home.

83. The download is finished. The monitor is small, so we have to sit close together. I hesitate going up next to the woman, afraid that she might smell. While I hang back, she comes up right next to me with her laptop. To my relief, she doesn't smell. She clicks on the movie file on the screen, saying it won the youngest best actor award at the Cannes Film Festival. She has already seen the movie.

"Why are you watching it again?" I ask.

"Because it's a good movie. And because it's been a long time since I saw it, and I've forgotten," she says.

The movie has a strong impact from the beginning. It starts with the director's words that it's based on a true story. It's a quiet movie set in midsummer, about four siblings with different fathers. I've downed two cans of beer so I should be getting drowsy, but I'm wide awake. Which proves that the movie is good. I focus on the facial expressions of the young boy, who won the best actor award at Cannes. I wonder whether the boy felt honored to receive the title of the youngest best actor, or burdened by it. I also wonder if the premature success and attention didn't actually hinder the boy's growth. Watching the movie, I ask the woman about him. He must've grown a lot, since the movie came out four years ago. I wonder if he's matured well. I'm curious as to his growth and development.

"I read an article that said he attempted suicide," the woman says.

I'm a bit shocked. The spotlight wears people out, puts them in a slump. Those who speed up too much from the beginning, without a gradual process of growth and change, become unhappy in the end, and at times, collapse to the point where they can't make a comeback. They may just use up their happiness in advance, like an advanced salary. If there's a fixed amount of happiness allotted each person, and the happiness could be allocated according to one's will, would it be better to place it early on in life, or later? If it were me, I'd place it later on in life.

Perhaps because I've learned about the boy's future, a dark shadow seems to cast itself over the face of the character in the movie. But no one could know why the boy attempted suicide. As the title of the movie says, nobody knows.

84. The impact of the movie lingers on longer than I expected. There's something about a movie based on a true story that doesn't let you to think of it as just a movie. When a movie starts out by putting brakes on the notion that movies are fiction, we grow nervous. This happens because there's a subtle but great gap between things that can happen and things that can't, and things that did happen and things that didn't. But at times, fiction becomes reality, and reality fiction. And at times, you just can't bring yourself to believe something that took place in real life— something you experienced firsthand, even—because it's so awful, it's something that happens only in movies.

The woman, who has the bed to herself, turns to face the floor where I'm lying and asks, "Does a postman really ring twice?"

"Three times, even, if there's no answer."

"Haven't you ever had doubts?"

"Huh?"

"About being a postman, I mean."

I think for a long time. Of course I've had doubts.

A great delusion I had about the job was that I could bring people happy news, and that I was a happy person for having such a job. Only after I began delivering mail did I realize that my belief was beginning to crumble little by little. All the mail in the world was divided into two kinds: auspicious mail bringing good news, and ominous mail bringing bad news. Loan repayment reminders, phone bill reminders, petitions and bills of indictment, requests for court appearances, notices of rejection, medical examination results, and so on.

I kept thinking that if people receiving such mail became unhappy, it would be my fault. This person won't be able to sleep tonight because of me; this person will have to put red stickers on his sofa in a few days, indicating that it was to be seized; this person will have to borrow money again from someone; this person will find out that a tumor is growing in his body; this person could hang himself or throw himself out the window because of me.

85. That was one of the reasons why I quit the job I'd worked at for nearly seven years. I said that the only thing I could do to minimize conflict with customers was not to make a delivery mistake, but in the end, I did make a mistake.

One day, with *Chuseok* approaching, there was a ton of mail to be delivered. There was a lot of registered mail, too. I had to keep walking up and down the stairs because I didn't even have the time to wait for the elevator. My legs ached, my eyes were dry, and I had a migraine, so severe that it felt as though my head would crack. Both my body and my mind were completely exhausted, and I had the last of the registered mail in my hand. I raised my arm and just barely managed to ring the bell. It was nearly evening, but no one answered, even after three rings. I had no choice but to put up a mail delivery notice on the front door, indicating that I'd return the next day.

The next day came, but I had forgotten completely about the mail. Something important—important enough to make me forget—happened to me, and I could no longer go on delivering mail. I requested a month of special leave at work. That one month, however, was not a break for me, but rather one long nightmare. Because of the seizures that came over me whenever I was at home, I had to spend the month going back and forth between my friend's house and mine.

It was when the month's leave was over and I was rushing to get ready for work that I remembered the registered mail. I felt something hard in my inner jacket pocket. I was so astonished that my forehead broke out into a cold sweat. Hastily, I drove over to the house on my motorcycle. There was no way that the notice would still be on the door, but I looked everywhere, in case it had fallen to the ground. The notice must've gotten lost, I thought, because if they'd seen it, they would've called, at least. I frantically rang the bell. There was no answer this time, either. I couldn't just wait forever, so I rang the bell of the house next door. The door opened, and out came a middle aged woman with a cast around her neck.

According to the woman, the addressee of the mail had moved. There had been sounds of quarrel for several days, and then the addressee slashed her wrist in the bathroom. Luckily she survived, but she could no longer move one of her arms. When I heard that, I wondered if it hadn't all started with the mail. The woman grew edgy because the mail didn't come; she threw a sock, turned inside out, at her husband's face; the husband broke the glass from which he was drinking; the question of the husband's ability to earn a living rose to the surface; the woman's past affairs shook up the night air; something in the house broke every night . . . and she slashed her wrist.

"You can't be sure that it was because of the mail, though, can you?" the woman asks.

"No, but the butterfly wings didn't stop flapping," I say.

It's difficult to unthink a thought you already had. Just as a hole is created the moment you drive a nail into the wall. I began to have doubts about my job, and submitted a letter of resignation as soon as I returned to the post office. Even if it weren't for the incident, I was already exhausted from many things. In the end, the butterfly which I thought made the woman slit her wrist made me quit my job as a postman.

"But on the other hand, there could've been someone whose life was spared thanks to the mail you delivered promptly. Everyone makes mistakes. The problem is when they repeat the same mistake over and over again. If the mail was important, she would surely have made an effort to find it. Think only good thoughts. Think about the good things the job has to offer," the woman says.

The words bring me some comfort.

I thought about many things on my way home from the post office that day. The many things I had gone through while delivering letters passed through my mind one by one, like scenery passing the window. I realized then, that just as you don't drink much liquor when you run a liquor business, and don't eat much ice cream when you run an ice cream business, I hadn't written many letters since I began delivering letters. After I decided to go on a journey, I resolved to write, as I traveled, all the letters I had put off writing. I decided that since I had spent seven years going around delivering letters, I should now go around writing some. And that my journey would be a journey of words, and a journey of letters.

I look up at the bed. The woman has fallen asleep. I look up at the ceiling. I'm blinded by the fluorescent light. I have the odd sensation that the light is interfering with something. Should I try turning it off? I get up quietly, and push the light switch. Sublime darkness falls. I lie down next to Wajo and blink my eyes a few times. A motel room with lights off. This is a first. The darkness is easier to bear than I thought.

86. The woman suddenly enters the bathroom as I write a sentence on the underside of the Motel Banana sink, my body crammed below. Taken by surprise, I bump my head against the sink. Curious, the woman squats down like me and sticks her head in.

"'Wajo and I were here?'" she reads.

She gets up, turns on the faucet hard, and washes her hands.

"I was here, too. How come I'm not included?" she asks.

Instead of wiping her wet hands on a towel, she deliberately shakes them off in my direction. Drops of water splash onto my face. She seems angry.

"This sentence has never changed in three years," I say, wiping my face.

I'm a little annoyed, too, because she won't be satisfied just sharing a room with me, but tries to take over my sacred ritual as well. She slams the bathroom door shut and leaves the room. She's really getting upset over nothing. It turns out that she's quite petty. I thought she was cool, so I'm disappointed.

"You're really petty, aren't you?" I ask, quickly catching up with her.

"I can put up with a lot, but there's one thing I can't tolerate," she says, stopping in her tracks and turning around to glare at me.

"What?" I ask.

"Being left out. Being excluded when I was there, too. I've always been alone, you know, and I like being alone. Sometimes,

I get up the courage to join other people, too. But they don't acknowledge that I'm there. It always happens to me for some reason," she says.

I've had similar experiences myself. My name would be excluded from the address section in the yearbook, a professor would remember everyone's face except mine, and so on. And the countless mistakes in recordkeeping that often occurred on paper. Whenever such things happened, I would cry out in my mind: Why me? Why do these things keep happening to me? Why me, of all the people in the world? I get left out. My life gets left out. When you're left out over and over again, you come to feel that you're left behind.

As one who's had similar experiences, I can understand how she feels being left out. Still, I can't quite figure out where she's coming from. I don't know whether she was being brave by correcting the omission, or arrogant by thinking she could interfere with someone's lifestyle just because she has shared a room with him. In any case, I'm perplexed, and feel that she has overstepped the boundaries.

"I understand. But consider the fact that this habit has been with me and these sinks for three years before I met you, 751," I say.

The discord arises from the fact that we require different amounts of time to accept each other. I need much more time than she does.

"I've never even been to a motel with a girlfriend," I say.

I don't know why I must divulge something so private to her.

"Yeah? That makes me feel even worse."

"I'm afraid that you've got the wrong idea . . ."

"What do you mean, the wrong idea?"

"You seem to think that we have some kind of a relationship just because we shared a room."

"You're the one who's got the wrong idea."

"What I'm saying is, I've done the best I could, and gone along with you. I mean, it wasn't because of me that we shared a room, is it?"

"So you're saying it was because of me?"

"Wasn't it?"

Now she's backing out. I think I've completely misjudged her. When things go wrong because of something so little, the idea of two is bound to become tiresome and annoying. I can begin to see why her friend pulled out a fistful of her hair while writing a screenplay with her. Absurd things happen at unexpected moments.

"I can see why your friend pulled your hair out," I say.

"What?" she says.

"You're making a big deal out of nothing."

"Look who's talking!"

"How can you write novels when you have so little empathy?"

"That's right, I have no empathy. That's why my novels are that way. You, 0, must have so much empathy, to wait three years for a letter that doesn't come!"

"W-what d-did you say?"

"You heard me!"

"How c-can you say such a thing?"

"You started it!"

"No, you started it! I'm really beginning to doubt your character."

"That's what I want to say!"

"You followed me around to save money on rooms, didn't you?"

"You finally figured that out?"

"What? A woman like you should live alone her whole life and die alone too!"

Wajo stands between us barking wildly, aware that we're quarreling. I decide that the time has come for us to go our separate ways. After all, until a just a few days ago, I'd been trying to come up with a way to part with her. Yes, this is great. It's a golden opportunity. I pull Wajo's leash and turn around in the opposite direction. The woman, too, goes on her way without looking back. I feel free. This is the way we split up. It's a little absurd.

I immediately found a mailbox and sent my letter, then called my friend. He got even more upset than I did, demanding why I was taking my anger out on him so early in the morning, and hung up.

87. No one wrote me.

88. A reply that doesn't come. If this, too, could be considered an omission, I was the one who was always left out by people. The pain of being left out, which I knew better than anyone, and felt more keenly than anyone. I come out of the phone booth and look at the asphalt stretching straight out to my right. The woman is nowhere to be seen. So, I fall behind.

89. The first thing that I notice after falling behind is an underground staircase leading down to the subway station. I'm a little surprised that there's a subway system in such a small town. Wajo and I walk down the underground staircase, curious as to what the subway in a small town is like. The people aren't busy, and it's quiet inside the station. I look at the subway guide map on the wall. There's only Line 1. Perhaps because there's only one line, the staff at the ticket gate doesn't stop Wajo from entering. I was prepared to plead with him to cut us some slack just this once, but it seems unnecessary. We decide to just wait for the subway, without pretending to be either a disabled person or a guide dog. I don't want to be left out anymore, not today. A disabled person is left out just by being disabled.

An hour has gone by, but we still haven't gotten on the subway. How many trains have we sent on their way, like the river? I was keeping count, but a thought interrupted me and I forgot. For some reason, I can't get on my way today. Is it because there's only one line? I wonder. Is it because I can't go far even if I get on, and can't transfer, either? I sit on the wooden bench staring at people, and get a soda from the vending machine when I get thirsty. While I do this over and over again, several more trains go by, but I don't remember how many.

I'm getting on the next train for sure, I decide, and go over to the vending machine with some coins in my hand. As one of the coins goes into the coin slot, the rest slip from my hand and clatter to the ground. I crouch down and pick up the coins one by one. One last coin sits still on a blackened piece of gum. I pick up the coin, and look attentively down at the gum. Thinking of 99, I scrape away slowly at the edge of the gum with the coin. I make an effort to scrape it off whole, stuck to the ground, but it's not an easy task. The gum cracks and breaks apart. Is it the tool? I move to a different spot and challenge myself to another piece of gum, but this one doesn't stay intact, either.

90. 99 was someone who scraped off pieces of gum with a flat tool, crouching down on the ground. Everyone looked at him with indifference as he cleaned the ground. They thought he was a street cleaner employed by the city hall. I did, too, in the beginning, but after watching him for a while, I realized that there was something different, something special about the way he carried out the task. He handled the pieces of gum with great care. The ones that didn't come off very well, he just put in a plastic bag, and the ones that came off intact, he put in a rectangular box as if they were treasures. He handled each and every one of them with concentration and care. I followed him around, waiting for his work to be done. He finally stood when it was dark, stretching out his stiff back with difficulty.

As he waited for the bus, looking over the pieces of gum in the box, I slid down next to him and said, "I followed you in secret because I was curious."

"I know," he said.

"You don't seem to be a street cleaner . . ."

"You can call me a street cleaner if you want. It does look as though I'm cleaning, and I was actually doing some cleaning."

Just as I was about to ask him an important question, the bus arrived and I followed him onto the bus without thinking. On the bus, he looked out the window without saying a word. He didn't even answer my question, as though he had set a rule that he wouldn't talk on buses. It didn't seem, though, that I was bothering him or making him uncomfortable. And somehow, I ended up going over to his house.

As soon as I entered his house, I could see what it was that he did. It seemed that he hadn't said anything because he thought it would be better to show me than to explain in words. To put a name to him, he was a gum artist. He was an artist who painted on round, flat, and worthless pieces of gum. Why pieces of gum, though? They had been chewed on and spat out by others, and trampled on and defiled by countless people. How had he come to use them as material for painting?

Sipping bitter coffee, he explained, "I loved someone once. She told me that I was like gum to her. 'Let's stay stuck together like gum. Will you stay by me all my life?' she said, telling me how she felt. I was like gum to her to the very end. This is what she said later on. 'You're really clingy, like gum, aren't you? I'm sick of you! Will you get off me now?'"

He emptied his cup of coffee with a bitter look on his face. It was the kind of expression I liked the most. For some reason I felt that someone who drank coffee with a bitter look on his face wouldn't lie.

He went on in an unaffected way, saying, "One day as I was walking down the street, I began to notice pieces of gum, thrown away after all the sweetness had been sucked out of them. There were too many of them. I haven't chewed gum since. Even if I did, I wouldn't spit it out on the street."

His works didn't look like pieces of gum at all. Each of them looked like a beautiful stamp. If they were actually cut out in the size of a stamp, with the perforated edges and all, there wouldn't be a problem sending letters with them. That's how incredible was the transformation of the black, filthy pieces of gum, which naturally led me to think that they were beautiful: 99, and the works created by 99. He promised me that he would send an invitation if he had an exhibition.

91. As I left 99's house at nearly ten in the evening, a question suddenly rose in my mind. What was true beauty? Was it beauty if you found it in something ugly and insignificant? If it were Jiyun, she would have answered in this way: What's really beautiful is a full bosom, an eighteen-inch waist, a high nose, large eyes that take up half the face, and a chin as sharp as an ice pick.

Jiyun was born with a great many talents. She got good grades, was very athletic, and was good at drawing and singing, too. She was truly well rounded. If my mother and brother were rational people, and my father and I romantic, Jiyun was a Renaissance woman. But she never did come into full blossom, or rise, or receive great attention or love from people as did the Renaissance.

Jiyun concluded that the reason lay in her appearance.

To Jiyun, beauty was another kind of talent. She believed that as a woman, if you didn't have beauty, you didn't have anything at all. Jiyun had often said that she wanted to be a woman who was envied and resented by people. But no matter how good her grades were or how good she was at drawing, the other kids didn't regard her with envy. She had to be good at such things for her not to be so pathetic and for her life to have meaning, they said, because she didn't have good looks, and she would have been the most obnoxious and hateful person in the world if she had been pretty on top of being smart.

What threw Jiyun into shock at once was an incident that occurred on White Day. The girl who always got the worst grade in class received candy, and the boy who gave her the candy was someone that Jiyun had a crush on. Jiyun realized at a tender young age: no matter how smart and talented you were, only a beautiful girl had the right to fall in love. After realizing that truth, Jiyun gritted her teeth to get into a good college. Once she was in college, she began to work as a private tutor and save money like a fiend.

One day, I asked Jiyun, who was lying on her bed after a nose job, "A-are you h-happy now?"

"I need thirty million won to be like Kim Taehee. I've spent only five million won. I want people to pounce on me, trying to destroy me. I read in a book that people try to destroy other people's looks, talents, or abilities because they're not things that can be taken away. But people aren't the least bit interested in my talents or abilities. Do you know why? Because I'm ugly. My talents get buried because I'm ugly," she said.

"Y-you'll e-end up d-destroying yourself th-that way."

"I don't regret it. Even if I end up dying."

It seemed that there was no one in the world who could change her twisted way of thinking. Jiyun became more and more beautiful, but more and more, she turned into someone I didn't know.

92. 99, who created original art using pieces of gum, and Jiyun, who loathed herself saying that she had breasts like pieces of gum stuck on the asphalt. On the street are two people I know, and their numbers are too many, and they are everywhere you go.

93. I hear the sound of a train approaching. This time, I must get on. I get up from my seat and walk up to the safety line. I turn my head toward the passageway from which the train is approaching. The wind blows, scattering my hair. At that moment, I see someone who looks familiar. Over in the distance, by the safety line, stands the woman. The woman is looking at me, too. She seems a little surprised. As am I. Our eyes meet for a moment. The train slowly comes to a stop, giving rise to a cool breeze. Will I get on, or won't I? The doors open. Will she get on, or won't she? I get on. The doors close. She got on as well.

94. The woman is in the first compartment, and I'm in the last. Because it's a small town, there aren't that many compartments to the train, and the aisle is so narrow that if you stretch out your legs, your feet will touch those of the person sitting across from you. I stand up and sit back down repeatedly. I make my way toward the first compartment. Just then, I see the woman walking toward me from the other side. I come to a stop. She comes to a stop as well. We're standing face to face in the central compartment of the train. She bursts out laughing first. I laugh with her. Thus we meet at the center of the train, both of us at the same time. It feels a little absurd.

"Why are you taking the subway?" she asks a little gruffly.

"Because it's the subway. Why are you taking it, 751?"

"Because I have to sell my books."

I recall how it was on the subway that I first met her.

I stare at the cart carrying her books, and say, "Can I try?"

"If it's because you feel bad, don't bother."

"Not at all."

I've seen people from speech schools, working hard to discipline themselves. They came out to the street in an effort to reform their personalities and treat their stutter. I usually came across them on the bus or the subway. But I never looked straight at them. I couldn't bring myself to raise my head because I felt embarrassed, as though I were seeing myself in the mirror. I would sit with my head bent low, glancing hesitantly at them once in a while, listening to what they were saying. A kid in middle school, much younger than myself, bravely talked about himself with clarity, and a balding man in his fifties took a peek at what he'd written down on a piece of paper and on the palm of his hand whenever he got stuck. He looked very strained and nervous, but he didn't give up until the end, and got off the bus after he'd finished speaking. To me, they were all great. They were putting into action what I was hesitant to do.

I'd always thought that the best place to put your confidence to the test was the bus or the subway. I, too, wanted to put myself to the test someday. After gaining confidence through my journey, I wanted the public to confirm that my stutter had indeed been cured. I'd sold books for the woman in the square, of course, but the people who had gathered there had come of their own will, out of curiosity. But with subway passengers, I couldn't tell what they were thinking because they couldn't leave their seats and run. If I could persuade with words those whose minds I couldn't read, I must have gotten better indeed.

The kind of person I consider the most courageous in the

world is someone who sells things on the bus or the subway, and someone who can sell things on the bus or the subway is someone who can overcome any trials.

95. Confidently, I go stand in the middle, pulling the cart. It's quiet and still on the subway, so I have no trouble getting the passengers' attention. I bow in greeting, and briefly introduce myself. Things are great so far. The response doesn't seem that bad, either. Next, it's time to advertise the book.

I open a book, and read a passage in a resonant voice so that the words may reach the people's ears. Like an actor on stage, I try to make the emotions come alive as much as possible as I read the dialogue. I seem like someone else, even to myself. What I'm doing is something that can be done only by forgetting and abandoning myself. The thought that I'm fighting a desperate fight penetrates every fiber of my being. The passengers must feel something, too, for they seem to pay greater attention to my voice.

When I finish reading, I close the book. Afraid that it might grow awkward if I stop here, I tell a joke and an amusing story. Then, before things cool off, I quickly start passing out the books to the passengers. Even after I return to my spot, I rattle off the random things that come to my mind so that things don't die down. I wonder if I look silly, and want to turn into a passenger and see how I look right now. I also wonder if I'm doing all right.

There was more I wanted to say, but the announcement comes on and the subway comes to a stop, making me stop midway. Why is one stop so short? The doors open and a throng of people get on the subway, creating a bit of commotion. At that moment, my eyes meet those of a woman with long hair who, having failed to find a seat, is reaching out for a strap. Her pupils grow large in an instant. The doors close and the train begins to move. She just stands there as though she has forgotten all about the strap. She doesn't lose her balance, even amid the rattling.

Standing face to face with the woman with long hair, I feel as if I've stopped breathing and turned into an ice statue. I feel thirsty and dizzy. I grab a strap in a hurry because I feel like I'll collapse if I don't hold on to something. The train speeds up. My body reels against my will. The reeling makes me forget momentarily about the task at hand. I even forget what I was doing here just a moment ago. The woman looks at me anxiously as though to ask me what's wrong. I finally come back to myself.

I swallow, say my last words to the passengers, and start walking stiffly to collect the books. I pass the woman with long hair, and pass her again on my way back. From somewhere comes the smell of coffee. A number of books are collected, and a number of bills come into my hands. But I can't tell how many bills there are. That's not what matters right now. I pull the cart and go sit down next to the woman. From the other end, the woman with long hair is still staring at me.

"Mission accomplished. You didn't stutter once," the woman says, taking the books and bills from me.

Breaking out into a cold sweat, I say in a trembling voice to the woman who's counting the bills, "L-let's g-get off at the n-next s-station."

"Why are you stuttering? Are you tense?"

"L-let's j-just get, off!"

"What's wrong, when you did so well?"

The announcement hasn't come on yet, but I leap to my feet and go toward the door, dragging Wajo with me. Why is one stop so long?

96. I leap out like a spring as soon as the doors open. The woman comes out after me. I feel like I can finally breathe. At that

moment, however, a voice behind me yanks at me. I remain still for a few seconds as if I've been caught doing something bad, and turn around slowly. She's looking at me with an incredibly bright smile on her face. Her gums never showed, no matter how brightly she smiled. She looks like an illusion, or a vision.

"Jihun? It's you, Jihun . . . isn't it?" she asks.

Her bright smile loosens up my stiff body in an instant. As though to tell me that she's neither an illusion nor a vision.

"Why are you running away? It's . . . it's me who should be running," she says.

Why am I running, indeed? Just as she said, she's the one who should be running, and I should be running after her to catch her. How I'd missed her. How I'd searched for her once. Why was I running like a coward when she, whom I couldn't see no matter how I longed to see her, was right before my eyes? It's probably because it's so unexpected. I'd never imagined that I'd see her again, and on the subway, no less, in this little town I'd never been to before. Sometimes, dramatic situations happen in the most unexpected places.

Her face, looking at me, is full of questions. My mind is full of questions as well. But the subway doesn't seem to be the right place to ask and answer those questions. We start walking toward the exit at the same time.

She asks cautiously, "Are you busy?"

"No, not at all. Not at all."

"What are you doing here?"

"Traveling. What about you?"

"I came to stay for a bit at my cousin's."

Our conversation isn't awkward at all. The three years' gap dissolves in just ten minutes, as if we saw each other just yesterday. As if it's only natural. It's an incredible phenomenon of time. Once above ground, she takes the lead, walking vigorously, as if she's lived in the town for a long time.

"Should we go for some coffee? There's a good coffee place around here," she says.

"Coffee?"

"You liked coffee, Jihun, didn't you?" she asks.

I nod my head quietly and follow her. And the woman follows me. The woman's face is full of questions, too. I hand her Wajo's leash and ask her to watch him for me for a little while.

"Who is she?" she asks.

"I'll tell you later," I say.

97. We walk into a quite large and luxurious coffee shop. The woman takes Wajo to a corner seat across from us and turns on her laptop. She's going to work on her novel.

"What shall we have today?" the woman with long hair mumbles, as though we had coffee together just yesterday.

I always left it up to her make the selection for me. The first thing she always said, looking at the menu, was "What shall we have today?" It's astonishing how she hasn't changed at all. It makes me a little angry. If she had changed even a little, I could think of her as someone else. The coffee she selected for me was always perfect, like magic, for the weather or the way I was feeling that day. I'm sure it'll be the same today.

I actually don't like coffee. Before I met her, coffee was a drink that had a completely different flavor and aroma. It smelled very good, but tasted like bitter Chinese medicine, not at all like the aroma I knew. It was something I drank only occasionally, not for its own flavor, but for the sugar. I came to acquire a taste for coffee after I met her, but after we broke up, it once again became something I drank only occasionally. That's what it means to break up. To go back to the way you were before you met someone.

After we place the order, she stares at me intently and asks, "How have you been?"

She's probably asking how I've been since we broke up. She'll feel hurt if I say I've been well, and sad if I say I haven't been so well.

"So-so. What about you?" I say.

"Same here. By the way, you were selling books on the subway, weren't you?"

"Yes."

"So I wasn't mistaken. Didn't you say earlier that you were traveling?"

She looks worried, probably thinking that I've resorted to becoming a salesman because of financial difficulties.

"I was helping someone out. Selling things on the subway was something I'd always wanted to do, you know," I say.

"I remember. It was because of your stutter, wasn't it? Hey! You don't stutter anymore, do you?"

"No. Not anymore."

It seems that, unlike me, she's taken by the new me. Would she not have run away if I hadn't stuttered back then? I wonder, looking at her sparkling eyes. Perhaps I want to blame her leaving me on my stutter. I could understand if that had been the reason for her change of heart. It would be difficult for anyone to love a stuttering man for a long time.

When the Yemen Mocha Mattari we ordered is served, she explains that it's also known as the "van Gogh coffee" because his hardcore fans drank it often, wanting to connect with him. There's a cup of coffee and some toast on the table where the woman is sitting. She feeds Wajo a piece of toast, then looks at me as she takes a sip of her coffee. She might be glaring at me. Then she begins to tap away at her keyboard. A coffee shop is a romantic place to write a novel in.

"So if you're traveling, what about your job?" the woman with long hair asks.

"I quit."

"When?"

"Around the time we broke up."

"Was it because of me?"

If I said yes, would she feel a little guilty?

"I had some problems, and couldn't go on working."

"Three years . . . So you've just been traveling all this time?"

"Yes."

"So you didn't get married?"

"No. Did you?"

"I did."

I nod my head quietly, as if to say I'd expected it. I drink my coffee, having nothing more to say. The coffee is bitter. I'd expected it, but I do feel a little sad. It feels as though she really did abandon and run away from me. Her choice, as usual, was excellent. She had ordered a coffee with such a flavor, anticipating such a moment. The bitter coffee tastes of sadness. It's the flavor of van Gogh. After she tells me that she got married, all the questions I'd meant to ask her fade away. As if marriage were the end.

98. How much time has passed? I think I've had at least three or four cups of coffee. My ex-girlfriend gets up from her seat with her bag in hand, saying she's going to the restroom. The woman comes over to me, bringing Wajo with her, as though she's been waiting for the chance.

"Haven't you been sitting here for too long? My butt's getting numb. It's been five hours already," she says.

Has it really been that long? It doesn't feel like we've talked that much, but time flies.

"I bought this at the bookstore across from here. There's only a few pages left now," she says, showing me the novel in her hand.

Most of the pages in the book, quite thick, have been flipped over to the left. She's trying to tell me how much time has gone by. No, she's warning me, in a classy way, that I should get up from my seat before she finishes reading the novel. Still, I don't think I talked that long; I think she just read at an abnormally fast rate. At that moment, my ex-girlfriend returns to the table. The woman hurries back to her own table with Wajo.

"Who is she? I've been wanting to ask. You were with her on the subway, too, weren't you? Is she . . ." she trails off.

"No, it's not like that."

"Then what?"

Could it be that she's jealous? But she's married. Should I just say that the woman's my girlfriend? So that she, too, would have closure?

"I met her while traveling," I say.

Am I still hoping for something?

"What about the dog?" she asks.

"That's Wajo."

"So that's Wajo?"

She's never met Wajo. She's only heard of Wajo's history from me.

"So you're traveling with Wajo. It must be hard," she says.

"Hard for Wajo," I say.

I finish the remaining coffee. The dregs have settled to the bottom.

"I'm hungry. Do you want to go get something to eat?" I say, putting the cup down on the saucer with a clink.

I glance over and see that half the coffee still remains in her cup. She never leaves her coffee unfinished. Like Turks, she always tried to read her fortune for the day based on the pattern of the dregs at the bottom. She used to read my fortune that way, too. That's why I couldn't leave my coffee unfinished when I was with her.

I say as though to correct a mistake, "I forgot. You have to read your fortune, don't you?"

She looks touched that I haven't forgotten her habit. Despite my thoughtfulness and concern, however, she gets up from her seat.

"I don't want to know my fortune today," she says.

When I raise my eyebrows, she says as though to correct herself, "Actually, I don't do stuff like that anymore."

"How come?"

"Because I don't think it works."

99. Once again, she takes the lead. The place specializes in pasta. Coffee and dinner. It feels as though I'm back in the days when we were together. I feel a flutter in my heart, though not as intensely as I used to feel. Does she feel the same way? I wonder. Regardless of being married, I mean. I want to find out how she feels, but I can't. She's married. The moment I find out how she feels, this sweet night out will turn into a sordid affair.

After the meal, we make our way over to a quiet bar. She was the one who suggested we go for a drink. It seems that she's changed a little, too, since I last saw her. At last, I'm beginning to detect the changes one by one. In the past, she couldn't drink at all. No, no one could stay the same always. Not in the face of time.

"I prefer beer over coffee now," she says.

"Are you still running the café?" I ask.

"No, I wrapped that up a year ago."

"Why?"

"Because I wanted to study."

"Study what?"

"Coffee."

She was a skilled barista. It seems, though, that even an expert like her has more to study.

"Why do you prefer beer when you want to study coffee?" I ask.

"I don't know," she says.

I met her while delivering mail. She was someone who brewed coffee at a café and waited every day for a letter from her sweetheart, and I was someone who delivered the letters she awaited. The letters from her sweetheart came by air mail, and her letters, too, reached the man, who was studying abroad in England, by air mail. She used to sit by a café window, drinking coffee and writing letters. Whenever she took a sip, the silver stud on her red tongue glittered alluringly.

For a long time, I watched their romance with pleasure. In today's world of e-mail, it was unusual to see people who wrote letters. In addition, their letters weren't the kind that could arrive overnight. They had to persevere, anticipating and waiting longer than did others. That alone made me feel that their love was different, and special. I thought I was one of the people cheering them on.

She gave me a cup of coffee as a token of gratitude whenever I delivered her a letter. She also gave me a cup of coffee when she gave me a letter to be delivered to England. So I was a walking mailbox for her. It was a pleasure to be a mailbox for her. Drinking coffee was a pleasure, too, so the first time she asked me if I liked coffee, I declared that I loved it, as if I had a taste for coffee. I think anyone would've done the same.

100. Then one day, I began to notice that their correspondence was growing few and far between. Even when she sent a letter, he made no reply. He was telling her that he was breaking up with her by not writing back. Around that time, her anticipation for me grew more desperate, and I felt bad whenever I went to see her empty-handed. As if it were all my fault. She no longer wrote letters, either, probably tired of waiting for a reply. Thus they broke up without a word. After that, another stud was added to her tongue.

I wanted to comfort her in my own way. When I had some time left after my rounds, I would stop by her café for a cup of coffee. She gave me coffee on the house even though I no longer delivered letters to her. It was like a habit. A habit is something more mysterious and confounding than affection. Affection is a conscious thing, but habits are subconscious. I thought at the time that perhaps what's real is dominated by the subconscious.

As if out of habit, we sat talking for half an hour almost every day at her café. I even made up an excuse to frequent the café, saying that I just couldn't do my job without drinking coffee because I got drowsy, when in fact, the coffee made my stomach burn like crazy. I thought being a postman was an awful job that didn't give you the time to go out with girls, but ever since I got to know her, I even came to think that there was no better job. I could develop feelings for someone, and could even go talk to her and have coffee with her while on the job. When I thought about it, the relationships I'd had before I met her lasted six months at most. The short moments we spent together led to a short relationship.

She once said to me, "Do you know that people look their sexiest not when they've taken off their clothes, but when they're concentrating on their work?"

"Huh?"

"You look sexy. When you deliver letters."

I couldn't really understand what she was saying. A postman could look sexy? But in my heart, I thanked my mother, thinking that I had the greatest job ever. Around that time, I was becoming louder and more talkative at home.

101. I admit now that as I delivered the letters, I always hoped that they'd break up. I'd never once cheered them on. Clutching their letters in my hand, I even cast an ominous spell on them.

I was probably jealous of the relationship they had. The kind of pure and noble relationship in which they sent each other letters by air mail. Writing letters was something I was also good at, so I probably wanted to be someone who wrote her letters, too. Perhaps I thought that I was the only person who could make the right kind of reply to her letters.

To tell the truth, I'd even snuck peeks at their letters. I was so curious about her private life and thoughts and sentences. I had to know about the man she liked, about his thoughts and personality and character. I completely abandoned my calling and conscience as a postman to be in on their secret. Solely for her.

102. She downs her beer in one gulp and says, "I called you once, you know."

"When?" I ask.

"A year ago. I couldn't reach you. And no one knew what you were up to."

"That's because I was traveling."

Why had she called? I wonder.

"Why did you call?" I voice my question.

"No reason," she says.

An uninspiring answer. I shouldn't have asked.

"Do you still have the studs on your tongue?" I ask.

She sticks her tongue out and waves it around to show me, and says, "Nope."

Another change I detect in her: When she drank coffee, the studs used to clink against the cup. I liked the sound, and even counted in my mind to see how many times the sound repeated itself while she drank one whole cup of coffee. It was the studs that made me want to kiss her, too. How would they feel against my tongue? I wondered. Would they be cold, or hard? When I kissed her, the first thing I did was feel for the studs. They were neither cold nor hard. They were warm and sweet like her tongue. They also tasted of bitter coffee.

Her cell phone rings. She takes the call without going outside. It must be her cousin. She's quite drunk.

"I'm with someone," she says to her cousin, looking at me with her face flushed, and says, "I don't think I'm going home tonight."

103. Being drunk, she has a hard time keeping herself steady. It's pretty late. The woman and Wajo, following behind me, seem very tired, too. She'll sober up once we go inside somewhere and rest for a bit. Helping her along, I head toward the closest motel, without a thought to the cost. The building is quite big and luxurious, compared to the motels I've been staying at. We walk past the rope curtain hanging at the motel's parking lot entrance and walk in through the door. As soon as he sees us, the receptionist throws us the worn out question. The question is the same, despite the high cost and quality. Today, however, the question sounds scathing somehow.

"We're staying the night, so give us a room, please," I say.

"One room? You're all together, right?" the receptionist asks, looking a little awed. For a moment, I'm confused as to what he means, and I realize that in tending to my ex-girlfriend, I had momentarily forgotten that the woman and Wajo are behind me. A man who says he'll stay with two women. The woman, probably embarrassed, steps forward and gets a separate room for herself. Having signed the card reader and taken the card key in her hand, she goes up to the second floor with Wajo. My room is on the fourth floor.

104. I get off the elevator and walk up to the door to Room 403. I slide the card key through the thin slot and the door glides open.

I stick the card key in the key tag on the wall by the front door, and a soft light comes on in the room. I take my shoes off, and enter the room and put my ex-girlfriend down on the bed.

It feels strange. I'd never been to a motel with her during the two years we were together. It feels disturbing somehow to be in a motel room with an ex-girlfriend, an ex-girlfriend who's married, at that. There are five condoms in a little crystal container on the bedside table. My heart thumps, as though they're egging me on. I put the condom container away under the bed as though it's something sinister. She tosses and turns at that moment, beating on her chest, looking tormented. She must be feeling sick. I'm about to get to my feet, thinking I should go buy some medicine, when she runs to the bathroom with her hands covering her mouth. I hear her throw up as soon as she's inside.

"Are you all right? Do you want me to pound you on the back or something?" I call out.

Instead of pounding her on the back, I knock on the bathroom door. The door is locked. After quite some time, I hear the sounds of the toilet flushing and the sink faucet being turned on. Then the faucet is turned off, and she comes staggering out of the bathroom and collapses onto the bed.

She looks up at me with unfocused eyes, saying, "You've never seen me like this, have you? How embarrassing."

"Well, you didn't drink back then," I say.

"Why won't you ask?" she suddenly asks in a cold voice.

I sit down, leaning against the bed, not having the courage to face her.

She asks me again from behind my back, "You know you have something you want to ask more than anything. Ask me why I ran away back then without a word. Go on."

She's not just asking, but insisting. The sound of the latest hit song comes flowing in from the corridor outside the door.

105. Our relationship ended because she broke it off. Or I should say, my relationship ended. I went looking for her everywhere, but she was nowhere to be found. I wouldn't have felt so frustrated if I at least knew the reason, but she didn't tell me anything, other than telling me in a letter that she wanted to break up. She was irresponsible, and I felt as though I'd been hit by a bullet. That letter of farewell was the only letter between us. It was a letter that required no reply, a letter to which there could be no reply. I realized for the first time that there are one-way streets even for letters.

It was odd, though. Why wasn't I asking her the question, when it was the first thing I'd wanted to ask if I ever ran into her, the first thing I'd wanted to find out? Was it because she was insisting that I ask? Would I have stepped up and asked, if she hadn't insisted? She answers the question anyway, since I still don't ask her when I've been given the time and the opportunity.

"I got a letter from the guy who was studying in England. He wanted to get back together. He said we could see each other soon, when he was done with his studies. Maybe I'd been wanting to get a letter at the time," she says.

Would we not have broken up if we wrote each other letters? Being with her, I forgot all about the existence of letters. I thought letters weren't necessary, since we saw each other every day. But perhaps letters were even more necessary because we saw each other every day.

She loved to write things down. Even when she was sitting at the café chatting with me, she constantly wrote things down with one hand. At times she wrote down key sentences from what I was saying, and at times, she scribbled down her own thoughts. I loved to see her writing things down, and I would just look at her, smiling. I felt that she, more than anyone, loved and appreciated her own memories. I also felt that someone like that would respect and cherish the thoughts of others. So perhaps for her, letters should have been a part of daily life.

"We began to correspond again. Through e-mail. But there was no sense of anticipation in waiting as there had been in the past. I just felt that things were being rushed. Maybe that's why I married him as soon as he returned from studying overseas," she says.

She heaves a long sigh. The hot breath reaches my back. I feel thirsty, so I walk over to the minibar and open it. There are two bottles of water, and three canned drinks. I take out a soda and gulp it down.

She waits for me to finish the soda, then goes on, saying, "And then I got divorced within two years."

Not having expected that at all, I quietly lower my head and crush up the can. I hadn't expected it, but I feel a little sad. In a way, I feel even more awkward than I did when I heard that she'd gotten married. Because a divorce meant that she had been unhappy. It didn't mean, though, that all the questions I'd prepared to ask her came back to me. As though a divorce meant the end.

"You resented me a lot, didn't you?" she asks.

"No, I was grateful to you."

"For what?"

"You wouldn't understand, but I could go on living because of you."

"What do you mean?"

"I mean that I'm breathing right now because of that letter you sent me, saying you wanted to break up."

"A kind of hatred, you mean?"

"A kind of irony."

She's probably staring at my back right now with a look of irony on her face.

She remains silent for a long time, and then says, "It's a good thing. That I got to see you like this."

"Yeah, it is."

"I'm going abroad. To study coffee."

"When?"

"When the summer's over."

" . . . "

We're both quiet, as though there's nothing more we want to say, and nothing more we need to say. She gently places her hand on my back. The hand is warm, but apologetic. I turn around and look at her. She's fallen asleep. I push the light button on the remote control and turn off all the lights on the ceiling. I am no longer afraid of the dark.

106. I open my eyes at the sound of someone knocking on the door. I glance at my watch and see that it's already eleven in the morning. There's a blanket covering my body. I don't see her. Instead, I see a letter sitting on the bedside table, like a lady sitting demurely with her hands clasped together. I unfold the letter and read it. The letter reminds me of a quiet dawn. I can imagine what she was thinking and feeling as she filled up the page with sentences. She has left, having written down in a letter the things she hadn't been able to say.

Once again, I've received a letter of farewell from her. A letter that required no reply, a letter to which there could be no reply. The first letter I've received on my journey. A letter written by her, not me, in a motel room. In the end, I remain someone who hasn't written her a single letter. When I realize that, I feel that for me, she has never existed at all.

107. I come out of the motel room. The woman and Wajo are waiting for me in the first floor lobby. The woman seems to be looking for my ex-girlfriend. I return my card key without saying anything to her and come out of the motel. She seems a little hesitant to talk to me as well. I just walk on. Even as I walk, all I can think about is my ex-girlfriend. I recall everything from the moment I ran into her on the subway to the last letter she left me. This is my last recollection of her. And my last show of respect for her.

"Did you guys catch up?" the woman asks.

"Just to let you know, she . . ." I begin.

"You don't have to say. It's not something you need to tell me, anyway. So your wish came true, didn't it? You finally got to go to a motel with her."

"Nothing happened."

"I didn't say anything. Who asked?"

"Well, I . . ."

At that moment, a feeling of emptiness courses through my entire body. The feeling, like blood, goes around every part of my body, and stops at my hands. My fingers wriggle involuntarily, and my hands get cold. Both my hands are sitting meekly in my pockets now, and the woman is pulling her cart with both her hands.

"Where's Wajo?" I ask.

"Wajo?" she says, looking around her in confusion.

"I handed you the leash as we came out of the motel," she says.

"When?"

I seem to vaguely recall being handed the leash. I let go of the leash to say goodbye to my ex-girlfriend. I look down in vain at my large palm. I see the pale face of my bedridden grandfather on the palm, glaring at me. I put Wajo in the woman's care all day yesterday, and never once gave him a pat. I didn't even feed him myself. It was the first time that I slept apart from Wajo.

"You let it slip out of your hand thinking of that woman, didn't you?" the woman scolds me severely.

She begins to run, calling out Wajo's name, before I do. The wheels of the cart bounce up furiously into the air. It looks as if Wajo were her dog. Coming to myself at last, I begin to run as well, calling out his name. My heart is pounding, about to be torn to pieces. He can't even see, so how anxious he must be, wandering around without me? He hasn't been hit by a car, has he? I comb the street with the ominous thought running through my mind. To my relief, Wajo isn't on the street. That's a good thing. But in a moment, an even more ominous thought weighs down on me. It would be worse if someone took him or a kennel man spotted him. What's more, it's summer now. Like a tsunami, all kinds of thoughts wash over me, and I'm so scared that my body begins to convulse. Wajo is probably even more scared than I am.

I come to a stop in the middle of the street like a child who has lost his way, tearing my hair out. I have no idea which way I should go to find Wajo. There's no signpost anywhere. The sweat keeps pouring down incessantly, as though I am in a desert beneath the blazing sun. My two feet, helpless and lost, merely circle round and round in their spot like the needles of a broken compass. I hope Wajo is circling round and round in one spot, too, not knowing where to go, so that I may find him easily.

Finding a lost dog is more difficult than finding a lost child. No one pays any attention to a dog wandering around by itself. People think that it's natural for dogs to go around without their masters, that they're supposed to go around alone. I wish I were a dog. It would be easier for a dog than for a person to find a dog. They remember things more through their sense of smell than their sight. The human sense of smell is useless. Smell . . . !

108. I run in search of a smell. I am not a dog and can't trace Wajo's smell, but I do know where I can find it. The human sight isn't completely useless. Using that sight, I run toward the place where Wajo should be. I'm certain that Wajo knows where to go, too, and being clever, he must be circling round and round like the needles of a broken compass after his own smell. Wajo's signpost. A dog that has lost its sight moves according to its sense of smell, and becomes even more attached to its territory. I pray that he's where I think he is.

I arrive at the motel I stayed at with my ex-girlfriend.

He's here. I see him in a distance. He's crouching down at the motel entrance. It's a miracle. That's probably the spot where Wajo had performed his ritual of urination. My heart is relieved, and my eyes well up with tears. I run over and take him into my arms, and Wajo recognizes me at once. He recognizes me by my smell. He wags his tail and licks my face. He licks my sweat. He licks my tears.

I hold his face in my palms, the palms that had let him slip away. Then I look for a long time into the black eyes that can't see. There must be a very thick darkness, unfathomable to me, beyond those eyes. A universe where no star or moon rises despite its darkness. Now that I think about it, I'd never given his darkness serious thought, or made a genuine effort to understand darkness from his stance. But with those black eyes, he looks at my wet eyes in turn one after the other, as though he can see. The eyes can't see, but they can talk. The eyes can't see, but I'm in those eyes for sure, alive and breathing. He sees me, and knows his universe. I'm sure that a moon rises, and stars fall, in that universe.

Wajo looks at me without the slightest sign of hatred or resentment in his eyes. I feel terrible. His eyes seem to say that dogs do not know what hatred or resentment is.

109. I go back to where I parted with the woman. I wait for her with Wajo's leash wrapped tightly around my wrist like handcuffs, determined never to let him slip away again. Since she doesn't know Wajo very well, she'll need more time than I did to find Wajo.

An hour goes by, and then I hear the loud sound of a cart being pulled. The woman trudges along toward us, looking drained, then plops down on the hard ground when she sees us. I wonder if her hipbone hasn't cracked.

"Where did you find him?" she asks.

"The motel we stayed at today," I answer.

She quietly nods her head as though to say that she hadn't thought of that, then strokes Wajo's nape.

"Tie the leash around your wrist so that you never lose him again!" she urges.

I show her my wrist, on which the leash is wrapped like a handcuff. She slaps my wrist without mercy. I wonder if my wrist bone hasn't cracked.

110. The woman gets up as her sweat cools off. One of the wheels on the cart is broken, and the cart is tilted to one side. I remember how severely the wheels had bounced up into the air when she began running in search of Wajo. I think it'll be difficult to move around with the cart in that condition.

I go into a nearby motorcycle dealership and explain the situation, to borrow the necessary equipment. I also stop by at a hardware store and buy some new wheels. I replace the old wheel with a new one through a process of beating and tightening. I replace the other one, too, for balance. The other wheel looked just as unstable, all worn out.

"You must take after your inventor father," the woman says, quite satisfied.

I think I've paid her back for being concerned about Wajo and doing all that she could to find him. I still can't stand to owe her because my relationship with her began with a debt in the first place. She tries pushing the cart back and forth, and tells me happily that it feels much sturdier.

After returning the equipment, we head toward the bus stop, with the woman pulling the cart and me pulling Wajo.

111. The bus that had been running quite well, like a hare, suddenly slows down like a tortoise.

The woman looks out the window to see what's going on and says, "Should we just get off here?"

She pushes the bell without waiting for my reply. The driver opens the door for us because the stop isn't that far anyway. I end up getting off the bus, thinking I should since he opened the door just for us.

Swept up in the crowd, we walk aimlessly. Flags and banners are hanging on the green trees lining the streets, signaling an event. I hear the sound of gongs, which becomes louder and clearer as we continue walking. We follow a little street and turn right, and a big street appears.

Stages are set up here and there on the street, where cars have been restricted, and performers in special makeup and costumes are singing and dancing on the stages. The people are huddled around below the stages, and give rounds of applause in return for the free performances. Flags of all nations are fluttering in the sky like socks hanging on a clothesline.

112. There's a festival going on in the city. It's the kind of a festival you can see in any city. All kinds of exhibitions, events, performances, and food get people moving busily about. The events accompanying such festivals are all about the same, too. Cities themselves are all about the same. They're places with tall buildings, a great number of people, polluted air, and all kinds of noises that keep you from understanding what other people are saying. In these places, people run like hares, focused on just getting ahead. A slow tortoise could never win the first place in a city. A tortoise is a tortoise, and a hare is a hare. The only chance the tortoise gets to win the first place is when the hare slacks off. Like in the fable. Fables always speak the truth. It's a shame that no hare comes to the city just to slack off.

We go over to a booth where free face painting is provided. The woman points to her cheekbones, asking the painter to write "toothpaste and soap" on them.

"Are you going to sell your books?" I ask.

"It's a festival, after all. No taboos," she says.

I want to get a soccer ball painted on my face, but change my mind. It's easy to give it up because soccer balls are something a lot of people have painted, and I've seen a lot of people with soccer balls on their faces. I ask for the word "toothpaste" on the woman's face, "and" on Wajo's forehead, and "soap" on my face, in big letters.

113. Toothpaste and Soap walk side by side. Then they find a suitable spot and come to a stop. "Toothpaste" plays the harmonica, "And" stands in the middle with his tongue hanging out in the heat, and "Soap" holds up a book toward the people. People begin to gather one by one to see Toothpaste and Soap.

The catch in the speech of Soap must have lifted, for he begins to spill out words like a medicine peddler. I feel as if I'm possessed.

"Today, I ate toothpaste. Tomorrow, I'll eat soap. Why would someone eat toothpaste and soap? Aren't you curious? If you are, buy the book and read it. Ten bestsellers don't compare to this one book. You'll regret it if you don't read it. Your loss if you don't know about this book. This one book can turn your life around. If you're heartbroken, love will come your way, and if you're unhappy, happiness will come your way. This book is a cure-all. That must be a lie, you say? There's no such book, you say? That's why you should give it a try. You've got nothing to lose. If you read it and don't like it, you can take revenge by giving it a bad review on the Internet. There's not that many left now. Soon you won't be able to buy it even if you want to. Oh, all right. I'll give you a 20% discount on the remainder. Oh, and you can get an autograph, too. Toothpaste, who's playing the harmonica, is the author. You can even take a picture with her. You never know what's around the corner in life. You should get an autograph while you can, and keep the picture for the years to come."

Toothpaste says to me without moving her lips, "Not bad, you should go into sales later on."

Soap, too, replies without moving his lips, "You know that's what I'm planning to do. Open up a toy shop."

"No, you'd be perfect as an itinerant medicine peddler," she says.

People open up their wallets more easily than I expected. It's because of the festival. I feel a lot less nervous than when I was shouting on the subway. That's because of the festival, too.

A high school girl with braids asks me to take a picture of the woman and her together with her cell phone, then asks Soap in a bubbly voice, "What kind of a relationship do you have, Toothpaste and Soap?"

"A relationship between toothpaste and soap," replies Soap.

The girl with the braids says, "That's a good relationship."

114. There's only one book left now. The woman says she wants to keep it, even though we could have sold it. She hasn't finished her new novel yet, and probably wants to allow herself some time to finish it.

We go into a nearby restaurant to eat, with the paintings still on our faces. To my surprise, the proprietor of the restaurant, a woman, doesn't forbid Wajo. It's because of our face paintings. We're wearing a sign that says we're enjoying the festival.

Today, with the taboos lifted for a little while, is a day of festival for this city.

For the first time in a while, we eat to our hearts' content without worries, and plunge ourselves into the festival. We watch the performances at ease, follow the parades with much lighter steps, and applaud and cheer along with the others. We eat when we get hungry, drink when we get thirsty, and stop for a rest when our legs get sore. The festival continues, even when bright lights go on in every street, and the stars and the moon rise in the sky. When the sky hides its color, the festival turns into a festival for couples. There are couples everywhere, walking arm in arm. Today, even gay couples are standing confidently at the center of attention at the carnival. They all laugh to the point of debauchery. I feel that at some point, the laughter will turn into groans. After they eat and drink to their fill, the time will come for them to make love to their fill. The night has always belonged to couples.

As I walk, it suddenly occurs to me that this may be the last festival for us. Even a festival of madness is bound to end at one point. Only loneliness and emptiness remain after a riotous festival. When it's over, the taboos that were lifted like magic will return like magic. I can hear the hour of taboos approaching step by step from far away. A lunatic, unable to deal with the aftermath of the festival, may send down a punishment of taboos. A night of madness may drive someone to madness.

115. A festival has a way of stirring up a city and people. Couples, unable to hide their excitement, get busy looking for a motel. There's no empty room at any motel. The lights of the motel signs begin to go out one by one, before we can get there. The couples take up the motel rooms, just as they'd taken up the night of the festival. Because they're quick, and because we're not excited, we can't find even a shabby room.

The place we find after walking around and around a little alleyway is a *gosiwon*, with rusty water flowing down the wall. There would probably be an empty room or two here. *Gosiwons* today aren't literally places for people preparing for an exam. It doesn't matter, though, if this place is for people preparing for an exam. They probably lead shabby lives too, and all we need is an empty room.

We open the *gosiwon* door and enter. Fortunately, there's a vacancy. They don't, however, rent rooms for just one night. The dozens of rooms, crowded together as in a beehive, flanking a narrow corridor with a width of less than fifty centimeters, are all rented on a monthly basis. Can people even breathe in these rooms, crammed so close together? That's why there are some empty rooms left, because rushed couples wouldn't come to this place. Most of the residents here wouldn't have the leisure of mind to take part in the city's festival. Their most urgent priority is to lay down their bodies, crumpled and crushed up with hard work. To them, a festival means sleeping.

116. Living out on the street, you often come across people who virtually live out on the street as well. Come to think of it, I've met quite a number of people who lived in a *gosiwon*. Most of them were satisfied living in a little room in a *gosiwon*. It wasn't because they had no desire, but because they had very little desire. Someone who stands out particularly in my mind is 367. 367 was someone who said he was happy that *gosiwons* existed. They were cheap, and most importantly, great in number, and the number was on the rise. He felt relieved, he said, because it meant that the number of places that he could go to anytime, and that would receive him, was increasing.

"Isn't it incredible how they've divided up the space in a single building into so many rooms people can sleep in?" he said.

367 even went so far as to say that *gosiwons* were great buildings. He said that the truly great structures weren't buildings such as the Sagrada Familia Cathedral in Barcelona, but little *gosiwons* that could accommodate over seventy people; that the truly great architects weren't people like Antonio Gaudi, but the nameless people who designed *gosiwons*, because they knew about the smallest and largest spaces in which humans could live, and turned them into reality.

"Even a person with ninety-nine rooms sleeps in only one room. And even in that room, the maximum space he requires is only as big as his own body. The size of a coffin. A big room only makes you greedy. Because you keep making frantic efforts to fill it up with this and that. Death? When your room is small, you become familiar with death, and are no longer afraid of it," he said.

367 said that the most pathetic person in the world was someone who worried that he would die without having spent all the money he had. An even more pathetic person, he said, was someone who had a lot of money but ended his own life without having spent it all.

"People are greatly mistaken. Rich people who are depressed don't need psychiatric consultations or prescriptions. What they need is a *gosiwon*. Tell them to try it out for just one month. If they need something stronger, just send them to a homeless shelter. There are more such places than mental institutions," he said.

367 was also the first person I lied to. I thought he'd curse me if I told him that I was going from motel to motel when I had a 45 *pyeong* house, so I told him I had no home. It was the first time, too, that I didn't regret having lied. The address 367 gave me had the word *"gosiwon"* on it in quite bold letters.

117. After much convincing, we succeed in getting a room. The proprietor of the *gosiwon* used the word "exception" in lending us the room. We're not sure whether the word is normally used when you're trying to take something or get rid of something, but we walk through the narrow corridor into the room of exception, thinking it was possible thanks to the festival, which has lifted taboos.

It seems that this is the first time the woman has been to a *gosiwon*, too, for as soon as we enter the room, she says, "It's small." She probably means that it's smaller than the motel rooms we've stayed in. She looks around the room, sits down on the bed that I'm not sure can even be called a bed, bounces up and down a few times and says, "It's enough." She probably means that the room is big enough for the three of us to sleep in. I, too, take a good look around the room, which is too small for the expression, "look around," and drift into thought. It seems more intimate somehow, probably because it's small. At the same time, I feel that it's quite enough, and full. The space is big enough for you to sleep in with both your legs stretched out, to eat, to watch a movie on a laptop, to drink, to fantasize, and even to have sex. The space is also big enough, of course, to write a letter in. Perhaps it's the kind of a space where you should write a letter.

The woman, too, must have thought that it's the kind of a space in which you must write a novel, for she turns on her laptop. We each concentrate on our work in silence. I take out some writing paper from my backpack, put it down on my lap instead of on the floor, and start writing.

Dear Jiyun,

I wonder how much you've changed. Whenever I spend such a long time away from you, that's the first thing that comes to my mind. The first thing that worries me, I should say. I worry that I may not recognize you when I return home after my journey. Whenever you made a change in your face, or lost more weight, I felt as though I'd lost another piece of my only little sister. I think everyone else in the family felt the same way. How many pieces of her are left now? I wonder. What if there's not a single piece I remember? I grow more and more nervous.

Whenever I looked at you with worry because you were changing piece by piece, you'd ask me in a sharp voice, "Do you want to live with a pretty girl or an ugly girl? Answer that, with your hand on your heart." I couldn't answer. I'm a guy, after all, and it's natural for most men in the world to want to live with a pretty girl. I thought that might be why girls, by nature, want to be pretty. I understood you in that moment. You were just an ordinary girl making a dogged effort to be true to your nature.

But Jiyun, a lot of guys don't live to be true to their nature. In the same way, a lot of girls are not true to their nature. Your question was misguided. There are many reasons, and should be many reasons, besides looks when one person comes to love another. For those reasons, men and women live without sticking to their nature. Love that's based on looks doesn't last long. You know that now better than I do, don't you?

That's why I was opposed the first time you brought a guy home, saying you were going to marry him. I asked him, while you were helping Mother prepare dinner in the kitchen, why he loved you. The first thing he said was that it was because you were pretty. So I asked him again, if he wouldn't have loved you if you weren't pretty. He said, without even blinking an eye, that he probably wouldn't have. And then he asked me why I would ask such an obvious question, when I was a guy, too. So I asked him again, if there weren't other reasons. Because you were smart, for instance, or because you were caring, or because you were good at peeling apples, at least. I waited with great anticipation, but he didn't say a single word. He just looked over at the kitchen, looking hungry, as if no other reason were necessary. The bastard! As a brother, I can recount many things that make you attractive. That bastard didn't know anything about you. I wouldn't have gotten so angry if he had said at least one thing. I wouldn't have gotten drunk and punched him on the spot, either.

I was quite shocked at the time and told you to reconsider, but of course, you didn't listen. You were already blinded by love. But fortunately, just as I'd hoped, the marriage didn't happen. He was the kind of jerk who would cheat on you not with just another girl, but two, three other girls. You're much too good for a scumbag like him. I was relieved that you seemed to have developed better judgment after that when it came to guys, but was also worried because you seemed have become even more obsessed with plastic surgery.

I suddenly remember when you were little. You thought that you were adopted because you weren't happy with your looks. In other kids' cases, it's the parents who tell them that they were adopted, to punish them for being bad. You thought you were born out of wedlock, through the unfaithfulness of one of our parents, because unlike your brothers, you didn't look like either of them. In the end, everyone in the family had to take a DNA test to free you from your delusion. In any case, you were quite unusual. You even said that you wouldn't mind stuttering at all, if it meant that you had the kind of looks that didn't need altering. Like the Little Mermaid, who became mute in return for a pair of straight legs. Perhaps for that reason, you were the only one who wasn't ashamed of me. You never said I looked stupid because of my stutter, or told me to try to fix it. Because no one would know any better if I just kept my mouth shut. I think I talked the most with you, because I felt the most comfortable talking to you. I think I stuttered less in front of you, for sure.

Do you ever wonder, Jiyun, what you used to look like, or miss your old self? The first thing you did after getting a nose job, despite our efforts to stop you, was to rearrange the photo albums. With scissors in hand, you cut up all the photos with your face in them, and even burned up the photos of your hundredth day celebration and your first birthday party. You cut out your figure from family photos, using a knife, leaving no photo in the albums intact. Seeing what you'd done, Mother got upset and cried a lot, and Father drank, even though he never drank. They thought it was their fault that you'd become that way. I know, of course, that you knew how they felt, and suffered more than anyone because you knew.

We were crushed when all the photos disappeared. We could no longer see what you used to look like. There was nothing left for us to do but forget. We could only see the old you by digging through our memories, and we didn't know when those memories would vanish. The photos of you as a baby, crinkling up your forehead, you in elementary school, looking sweet and innocent, you in middle school and high school, when you looked somewhat gloomy, and you with the family, with a smile on your face . . . All of it was gone. I think you probably miss your old self more than any of us.

If you miss and want to see your old self, just let me know. Do you remember the photo of you, taken in the front yard in your high school uniform? It was summer, and the flower garden was in full bloom. It was a Saturday afternoon when the flowers were in their glory, and I felt an urge to take a picture of something, so I steered you to the flower bed as you stepped in through the gate. You fell on your rear end because I forced you in there when you didn't want to get a picture taken. But you got right back on your feet and shook off your skirt, and smiled an incredibly bright smile when I shouted, "One, two, three!" It was a clear, vivid smile. At that moment, you were so beautiful that you made the flowers in the background look shabby. I'm so glad I snuck that picture out of the album when you were undergoing surgery.

You probably don't look the way you used to, the way I remember, but you're my little sister no matter how much you change. Because you'll always go on caring about your family, caring about me, in your beautiful heart. What matters is an unchanging heart, right?

All I have for you is that one photograph. I hope you like it.

Your brother Jihun, from Hanbit Gosiwon

p.s. This place called a *gosiwon* . . . It's a place I hope you'll visit someday.

118. The woman is lying on the bed that can hardly be called a bed, and I'm lying on the floor, with Wajo, on the floor that can hardly be called a floor. The tiny window may as well not exist, so it's really dark when we turn off the light. It occurs to me that a *gosiwon* is place that makes you realize what real darkness is. It seems that the compulsion that used to come over me like a habit has lifted completely, for I don't feel afraid at all even when I've learned what real darkness is. I think I can endure any darkness now, for there couldn't be a thicker, vaster darkness anywhere.

"Are you asleep?" the woman says in a whisper, afraid that someone could hear her next door.

"No," I reply in a quiet voice as well.

"It's quieter than I expected."

"Everyone's tired."

"I wonder what they're all thinking."

"Tomorrow . . . They're probably thinking about nothing but tomorrow."

"It's a wonderful thing that you have a home to go back to."

"I know."

"What's the first thing you're going to do when you go home?"

"I don't know. I've never thought about it. What about you, 751?"

"I'm going to fix the bathroom faucet. I just took off, even when I saw water leaking drop by drop. It's probably leaking every five seconds, even now. That worries me once in a while."

"If it were up to me, I'd just leave it alone."

"How come?"

"Isn't it reassuring somehow, knowing there's something moving in the empty house? Plus, it makes you think of home once in a while."

"True. If it weren't for the faucet, I would've never thought of home. There have been times when I wanted to go home because of that. What else would there be that moves?"

"Clocks."

"I took the batteries out of my clock before I left."

"Don't do that the next time you leave. Even an empty house needs time. A tiny room, too, of course."

"Doesn't it seem like time doesn't exist here, when it's not even an empty house?"

"That's because everyone here is tired."

"I feel like I should try to look tired, even when I'm not."

"It may be the opposite, actually."

"What do you mean, the opposite?"

"It may be a place that makes you laugh."

The woman feigns a very quiet laugh and asks, "Like this?"

I say, "Yeah, like that."

And then I ask, "By the way, have you finished your novel?"

"I'm not sure," she says.

"What kind of an answer is that?" I ask.

"I've written and rewritten it again and again, but I still haven't come up with the final sentence."

"When you think about it, novelists are sorry people who must write all their lives to come up with just one great sentence," I reflect.

"Your life would be a success if you had just one sentence to carve on your tombstone. They say that Stendhal spent his lifetime searching for the sentence to carve on his tombstone."

"What was the sentence?"

"He lived, wrote, loved."

"Tombstone, huh . . . I wonder what mine will say."

"Take your time thinking about it. You've got many days ahead of you."

I think about telling her that no one knows for sure, that no one can guarantee it, but roll over without saying anything. I can feel Wajo's faint heartbeat through the floor that can hardly be called a floor. I close my eyes and try to sleep. I want to take my time thinking about such things.

119. Something soft and wet touches my lips. Is it her? I imagine for a moment, but it's Wajo, licking my lips frantically with his tongue. He whimpers, too, as though he wants to go relieve himself. A little annoyed, I open my eyes slightly and close them again, covering my face with my arms. Then I curl up so that my nose touches my knees. I'm stiff all over, and I have a slight headache, perhaps in the aftermath of the festival. Heedless of my condition, Wajo forces his head in between my arms, and starts licking my lips again.

I wipe away the sticky saliva with the back of my hand and say as if in my sleep, "If you want to go, go. I won't scold you."

Wajo lets out a fierce bark, and takes my arm in his mouth and keeps trying to drag me somewhere. I open my eyes. Wajo drops his tail to the floor and growls sharply. Then he spins round and round in his spot, making me nervous, and scratches the door with his paws. I thought I had sleep in my eyes, but no. There's a light fog in the room. I jump to my feet. It's neither sleep, nor fog. It's smoke. There's a fire.

120. Shouting, I shake the woman awake. I shake and shake her, but she doesn't get up. Something's wrong. I slap her on the cheek. She still won't get up. I sling her onto my back at the speed of light and slip our backpacks onto one arm. Then I take Wajo's leash with my other hand. I have no hand left for the woman's cart, standing next to the door. I decide to go without it. There's not a second to spare. We need to get out of here if we want to live.

I open the door. When I do, a thicker smoke blasts into the

room like the devil's shadow. Outside, it's already heavy with smoke. I can't see anything. Just like Wajo. The building is too quiet, as though no one knows there's a fire. It's peaceful and desolate, like a misty mountain. I look around, but there's nothing that looks like an exit light anywhere. No fire alarm sounds, either. As if to say that there's no way that there could be such a thing in a place like this. That there isn't supposed to be such a thing in a place like this.

Since there's no fire alarm, I shout "Fire!" and run toward the exit. The room of exception in which we were staying was at the end of the first floor corridor, so we'll come across an exit if we keep walking forward. I grope my way out as I continue to shout fire and knock on the other doors with the hand holding Wajo's leash. The smoke and coughing ruthlessly block out the shouting. The more I shout, the more I choke and no sound comes out. My lungs must be full of smoke, for I suddenly have a hard time breathing. I think I'll die without lasting thirty seconds in this condition.

The moment I feel that I'm at the edge of death, I feel a wet glass door right in front of me, like salvation. I open the door and come outside. I feel dizzy and collapse to the ground as soon as I do. The sky is dark and there's no one to ask for help. But the thought flashes through my mind that I can't just stay lying on the ground. There's no time. I get up and check on the woman. She still hasn't regained consciousness. The fire broke out on the fourth floor. I can see the flames swaying through a little window. I tie Wajo's leash to the woman's wrist and start going through her stuff. I feel the cell phone in her back pocket. I take out the phone and push 119.

121. There's no one else who's come out of the building. We can't just wait like this for an ambulance to come. Then suddenly, I remember the letter I left in the room. The letter for Jiyun, which I placed at my bedside before going to sleep. I hesitate. Should I go back for it, or not? Should I give it up, since I can write another letter anytime? No. Even if I do write another letter, I can't write it with the same feelings I had yesterday. The letter is unique, pertaining to yesterday. Thinking that, I feel as if I left Jiyun in the flames.

I take out a water bottle from my backpack and throw water on my sleeves. Then I cover my nose and mouth with the wet sleeves, and run frantically into the building. The smoke is thicker than before, and darker as well. I can feel the heat on my skin, too. I go back in the way I came out, feeling along the wall with my hands. I beat on all the doors, shouting fire. And then I hit my forehead against the wall at the end of the corridor. The pain tells me that I'm still here.

I go into the room on the right, and crawl on the floor fumbling for the letter. I feel a pain in my chest. I'm having trouble finding the letter. My eyes sting. I come across nothing but hard furniture. Tears begin to flow. Did I put the letter somewhere else? I start coughing. The sentences I wrote in the letter come to my mind one by one. The tiny room, which could easily be seen at one glance, now seems as vast as a desert. I try to remember everything I did after I wrote the letter last night. The memory, too, is unclear, full of haze. I move my hands with more deliberation. At that moment, the smoke that had been veiling my memory begins to clear, and I remember where the letter is. My memory tells me that it's at the edge of the bed. I can't die here. I feel along the edge and come upon something. I can't die here. Half the letter has slipped under the bed. I need to get out of here fast. Quickly, I pull out the letter with the tips of my nails. I can't die. I put the letter in my pocket and turn around.

Having barely managed to come out of the room, I open the door to the room next door and go inside. I can't see anything, but I'm sure there's someone inside. I grope along the bed, just as I did as I looked for the letter. I come upon a small foot. I go outside, carrying the stranger on my back. At last, people are starting to come out of their rooms one by one, shouting fire.

122. The day is dawning. The fire truck shoots up streams of water in all directions, but the fire doesn't die easily. The building probably wasn't constructed using costly materials, since the place is mostly occupied by those who are impoverished. So the flames won't be extinguished easily, and will die only when they've consumed everything and can't spread out any further.

People, covered in soot, come out with the help of the firemen. Some are carried out on a stretcher, covered in a white blanket. I don't know how many people are enveloped in those flames. I don't know how many people have made their way safely out, either. Who would know them, when they don't even know who lives next door? Those with unconfirmed identities can't have their identities confirmed even after death.

It occurs to me that all of this may have happened because of the festival. A young man got depressed, not having been invited to the city's festival. He must have felt even lonelier that usual, without friends, without a girlfriend, without a job, and without a home. To him, the night must have seemed colder and longer than ever. Sitting crouched in his little room with the lights out, he must have tried at first to endure through the long, long night with countless flights of delusion and fancy. The loneliness, however, must have continued to harass him, lying on one side of his little room, not leaving until the end, like an unwelcome guest. The more flights of delusion and fancy he had, the more miserable he must have felt. Unable to bear it any longer, he must have used a lighter to set fire to the clothes he had hung, like his soul, on the wall. There must have been no hesitation. Or trembling. Or fear. He must have wanted to throw his own festival, even if it meant setting himself on fire. Then he must have vanished, like smoke.

123. "Are you all right?" I ask.

"I just have a little headache. Thank you, for saving my life," the woman says.

"It was Wajo who saved us."

"He's better than two blind fools."

"I couldn't get the cart out."

"Who cares about the cart . . ."

She strokes Wajo's neck, and bursts out crying.

"I wonder how many people died."

"They found about seven bodies."

"I could've died."

"But you didn't."

"Seven people have died."

I look up at the building where the flames have now been quenched. It's an awful sight.

"They were so miserable, and now they're even more miserable," she says.

"The world . . . doesn't . . . cut you any slack because you're miserable. I'd say it treats you even more cruelly, if anything," I say.

We have a hard time leaving the spot, feeling sad for those who died, and guilty that we survived. Pain has come to an end for those who died, and has begun anew for those who remain alive. I don't know which is worse.

124. I see a mailbox in the distance. I finally remember the letter in my pocket. The mailbox stands firm and tall, like a mother

welcoming back her son. It couldn't look any sturdier. I'm happier than ever to see it, and even feel a desire to go up to it and hug the bulky body tightly in my arms and kiss it. Instead of hugging the mailbox, though, I take the soiled, crumpled letter out of my pocket and smoothen it out. Would Jiyun know? That a fire broke out and a lot of people died at the place where I wrote this letter? That I jumped back into the smoke to salvage it? That I was able to save a life because of this letter? No, that she, Jiyun, saved a life? The envelope smells like smoke, as if to say that it knows, even if Jiyun doesn't. I'm glad that I retrieved the letter. I put it in the mailbox, which is like a mother's bosom. I think it's safe there.

When I turn around, the woman hands me her cell phone as though she's been waiting. I take it without a word. I'm too drained to go looking for a phone booth.

The phone call with my friend lasts for quite some time. I tell him about the fire more vividly than a journalist, and he tells me he just read some related news on the Internet and asks me repeatedly if I really had been at the scene. He says there's never been anyone close to him who had been at the scene of such an unfortunate accident, and asks in a slightly trembling voice if I'm hurt in any way. He says he's scared, probably feeling that the news isn't just someone else's business, though normally, he wouldn't have given it a second thought. He wants to treat me like a hero, as people do with those who had a narrow escape from the scene of a fatal accident. He seems to feel the gravity of the situation more profoundly when he hears me cough as I talk. Until the moment we get off the phone, he says repeatedly in a genuinely concerned voice that I was lucky that things hadn't gotten any worse.

125. No one wrote me. My friend sounds more apologetic than usual as he tells me the news.

126. As I hand the woman her cell phone, I notice that she looks grave. I ask her if she's not feeling well. She shakes her head, and looks at Wajo.

"I think there's something wrong with him," she says.

Wajo is lying on the ground. I run over and get him on his feet, but his legs must be weak, for he drops right back to the ground. I take out a handful of dog food and put it to his nose. He turns his head away indifferently as though he doesn't even want to smell it. He closes his eyes gently, probably just wanting to get some sleep. Wajo is not the kind of a dog that goes to sleep sprawled out on the street. He never relaxes on the street because he still has a sense of mission as a guide dog.

"I think we should take him to a vet," the woman says.

I think the fire must have had some kind of a negative impact on Wajo. He seems a little short of breath, too. The woman hails a taxi. When the taxi comes to a stop, we get Wajo in it. The woman asks the driver to take us to the biggest animal clinic. Even in the taxi, Wajo keeps his eyes closed.

127. The vet asks me questions about Wajo and writes down the answers on a chart before he begins the examination. His age, the size of his meals, the kind of food he likes, the condition of his feces, his usual habits . . . I stutter a little in a trembling voice, and the woman steps forward. She tells the vet everything she knows about Wajo in a calm voice. She tells him that Wajo used to be a guide dog for the blind, that he hurt his leg in a traffic accident, and that he has lost his sight as a result of the accident. She doesn't leave out that he's been traveling for three years, and that he was at the scene of a fire. The vet nods thoughtfully at her words. The thought crosses my mind that she knows quite a lot about Wajo.

Various tests are conducted. Blood tests, x-rays, ultrasounds . . .

The vet doesn't look too happy as he comes out with the x-ray films and a stack of paper stating the results. My heart is pounding already, as if it's aware what kind of words will come out of his mouth. The vet places the x-ray films on the reader and calmly explains Wajo's condition. I can vaguely see Wajo's white bones and various organs on the white reader. The x-rays look neat and clean, like there's no problem at all, but the vet keeps saying it isn't so.

He says that Wajo, being an old dog, is quite worn out from the journey. His heart is weak, his liver is swollen, and his kidneys and prostate are somewhat problematic. The leg he hurt in the accident is arthritic, and the fire has put a bit of a strain on his lungs and bronchus. The functions of all the organs have dropped a little below the normal range.

"It would be best to let him rest for now. Let's inject him with some insulin solution and nutritional supplements for about half a day," the vet says.

He begins the treatment. A sharp needle is injected into Wajo's body, and all kinds of tubes that look like wires go up from his legs to the IV bag hanging in the air. The fluid drips down the tubes, like drops of water falling from a broken faucet. Wajo closes his eyes gently and falls into deep sleep as soon as he's injected with the fluid. His breathing grows more quiet and peaceful.

The doctor asks if I hadn't noticed anything different about Wajo, saying that he must've been having quite a difficult time, that in such a state, he must have shown at least one or two signs indicating something unusual, in his countenance or behavior. I just shake my head quietly. I did think that he'd grown weak, but he'd seemed pretty healthy in my eyes. He hadn't been healthy, though; he'd been trying to endure. If, as the vet said, Wajo had been telling me how he felt through his eyes and expression, and I'd been dragging him along everywhere without taking notice, thinking only of myself, how will I be able to convey my remorse?

"The journey must've been good exercise for him, since he can't see, but it must've become stressful with time, because of his old age," the vet says.

Wajo had endured for my sake even when he was exhausted, without letting on. Just to be at my side. He had thought only of me, not at all of himself. Perhaps Wajo still thought of himself as a guide dog. Or perhaps he had a sense of duty, feeling that he must be at my side protecting me until his life expired. Perhaps he thought it was because of him. As I did at first.

128. For Wajo, the journey must have been a pain. I gently take his bandaged paw in my hand. It's true that I've had a lot of changes in my heart since I met him. I learned for the first time, too, that an animal can change the way a person thinks. I once saw a picture. It was a picture of a girl in Afghanistan who had lost her parents in a war. The girl was staring at the camera with a starved look on her face, sucking on a dirty finger. Her pupils seemed to say that she didn't know whom to blame, and whom to hate. There was a filthy dog standing next to the girl. If I'd seen the picture before I met Wajo, I would, for sure, have felt sorry for the girl. The filthy dog standing next to her wouldn't even have caught my attention, and even if it did, I wouldn't have cared whether or not the dog starved. But oddly, that day, I felt more pity for that filthy dog than I did for the girl. My eyes stayed on the dog longer than they did on the girl. It was because I knew Wajo. I think the photographer who captured the girl and the dog in the same picture had the same belief I did: that whether dogs or humans, they were all living beings.

On my way out after seeing the picture, I tried to figure out the reason why my eyes had focused more on the dog than on the girl. I felt as though someone would point a finger at me if I didn't. And at last, I have found the reason: dogs have no language. They can't speak or write letters, or say they're hungry or sick. Human civilization was made possible through the existence of language. Language meant communication, and communication meant progress. Dogs could not establish a civilization because they did not have a language and could not communicate. I'm sure, of course, that dogs have their own way of communicating that can't be understood by humans. The problem is that when they meet someone uncaring like me, they can't communicate, and must suffer in silence for a long time. Dogs can read human emotions, but too often, humans can't read theirs.

My grandfather always said to me that dogs, who can't speak, are to be pitied more than are humans. That dogs are better than humans. He was right.

Without letting go of his paw, I try saying something to Wajo. Wajo says nothing.

129. It's past ten in the evening, and I come out of the hospital with Wajo in my arms. He must be very sick indeed, for he stays close to me like a baby, without struggling to get down. He feels too light. I look up at the sky. The night sky seems darker and vaster than ever. I don't even know where to go. Then the woman says we should get a room, since it's so late. With Wajo in my arms, I follow her to the nearest motel. She gets a room and pays for it. Somehow, I don't feel indebted this time.

130. The woman and I are lying down side by side, looking up at the ceiling, with Wajo between us. The days I've spent with Wajo pass through my mind like pieces of a puzzle. Wajo is in every one of them. Wajo, who had made me, as well as the people we met on our journey, laugh and cry. Three years. It certainly wasn't a short time. For Wajo, it must have seemed like a long, long time, like thirty years. It must have felt longer and farther away because he couldn't see.

It crosses my mind that what has made such a long journey possible for me was Wajo, not the letters I didn't get. I've been able to hold out for a long, long time because I had Wajo. I have truly enjoyed my journey with Wajo, and I wonder if he has, too.

The woman answers for Wajo, saying, "They say that dogs don't blame their masters for being poor. So they probably don't blame them for anything else, either. They don't complain or harbor resentment. That's the difference between humans and dogs. Dogs are content just to have a master. Even when they're hungry or sick. He must've enjoyed the journey thoroughly, since you two were never apart for three years."

"We were apart that one time."

"But I was with him."

I feel as though my time is up. I am witnessing the last grain of sand in a hourglass get buried and disappear amid countless other grains of sand. So I'm going to end this journey here. I'm going to end it for the sake of Wajo, who must have been tired and weary despite the good times. The journey, which in a way began with Wajo, comes to an end with Wajo. With Wajo, not with a letter, as I'd expected. That is the only act of consideration I can offer Wajo, and the respect he deserves. And in fact, I'm tired enough myself to put an end to this journey. It was a journey that had to end sometime. Just as everything comes to an end, my journey, too, comes to an end. It doesn't matter that I didn't get what I'd aimed for through this journey. I feel that the three years

I've had with Wajo are enough. The direction he chose has never disappointed me, so once again, all I have to do is follow him.

I recall the beginning of my journey, when I had no confidence and little knowledge of the world, and very little courage to stand up against it. My twenties, which I spent on the road, and my thirties, which I arrived at on the road. And now I'm at the end of the journey. Have I learned anything about the world? Have I become any stronger?

Tomorrow, it's time to say goodbye to the woman. It seems that our time together has been very short in a way, and very long in a way. The Savannah will be our last motel.

"I'm going home tomorrow," I say.

"You should. Wajo must be happy that he has a home to go back to. Do you know now? The first thing you'll do when you get home?" she says.

"It hasn't hit me yet. It's been three years, after all. I feel afraid, in a way."

"Of what?"

"Of whether or not I'll be able to adjust."

"What are you worried about, when you have your family, and Wajo?"

"You're right. And the clock must be ticking, too."

"And the water may be dripping from your faucet, like mine."

"What should I do then?"

"Just let it run."

" . . . "

131. I keep tossing and turning, unable to sleep. Is it because this is my last night, or because the lights are still on? Suddenly, the thought of a letter comes to my mind. I can't sleep because I haven't written a letter. The power of habit is great.

I lie face down on the floor to write a letter. From my backpack,

I take out some writing paper and a pencil with an eraser on it. The pencil has grown stubby. The eraser is worn out as well, with only a flimsy layer sitting atop the metal protection cap as if it's been sliced thin.

I write my last letter on this journey, pressing down so hard that the lead nearly breaks. My fingertips tremble a little, like a stutterer, at the thought that this will be the last. The letter is for Number 1, whom I met on the journey. A letter to 1, a fellow traveler who was with me on the first and last days of my journey. It feels as though the beginning and the end are intertwined, thus leading to a never-ending cycle. Surely this will not be the end. Just as it can't be considered the beginning. Just as it can't be determined where the beginning or the end is.

This night, on which I'm writing the last letter of my journey, is more sacred than any other. Wajo's breathing is as quiet and tranquil as ever. He doesn't bark once, as though he knows to whom it is I'm writing. When I have finished writing this letter, my hour will be 0 o'clock, and the hourglass will turn over.

132. Before I leave the room, I squeeze in my stiff body underneath the sink, and write a little sentence on it with a marker.

August 10, 2009. Wajo and I and 751 were here.

133. I go out of the motel, holding Wajo in my arms. The woman is waiting for me in front of the motel.

Tapping on the cement ground with one foot, she says, "I think this is where we should say goodbye."

I don't know what to say. Perhaps because there's too much to say, or perhaps because there's too little. In a way I feel like something should be said, and in a way, like nothing at all. After great hesitation and deliberation, I finally manage to come up with a single sentence.

"You're the first novelist I've met."

"It's an honor," she says, smiling brightly.

Then she stops smiling, and begins to tap on the cement ground again.

"Are you going to keep traveling?" I ask.

"I think I'll go home, too," she says.

"Does that mean that you've come up with the last sentence?"

"Yes."

"When?"

"When I came out alive from the *gosiwon*."

I'm curious as to what the sentence is, but I don't ask. I'm certain that it's a great enough sentence to carve on a tombstone, since it's one that was gleaned in the moment of death. I'll be able to see it in print before long, when the book comes out. She takes out a book from her backpack and hands it to me. It's *Toothpaste and Soap*.

"The cart . . ." I start.

"It was an empty cart. And I'd taken out in advance the last copy I kept for you."

"I want to buy it the proper way, like everyone else."

I reach for my wallet, but she stops me.

"I want to give it to you at no cost. We're Toothpaste and Soap, you know," she says.

"Thank you," I say, accepting the book.

To tell the truth, I've been wanting to read it as soon as possible because I, too, wanted to find out why the protagonist ate toothpaste and soap.

"So it turns out that you're the last person I met on my journey," I say.

"So it's not a temporary number anymore?" she asks.

I just smile.

"But I can't be the last . . . There's no end to numbers," she says.

"You're right. It's not the end," I say.

"This probably won't be the end for us, either."

"I'm sure you're right."

"Goodbye. And take care."

"You too, 751. Thank you for everything."

She pats Wajo on the head, bidding him goodbye, and starts to walk backwards, receding little by little.

Then she stops for a moment and says, "Thank you for everything, too."

"For what?"

"I mean . . . I think being with another person is all right, too . . . It doesn't seem so bad."

She beams, and resumes walking backwards. I'm about to say something, but stop myself. I'm about to say that I thought it was all right too, that it wasn't so bad, but don't. Because even if I don't, she probably knows already. Based on the fine tremor in my voice that must have occurred in our many conversations.

She raises her arms high and waves. I wave back. She puts her hands in her pockets and turns around. I turn around only after I see her turn around, looking a little lonely. Thinking back, I realize that of all the people I've met so far, she's the one who asked me the most questions. She's the one who listened to me the most as well, and the one who knew the most about me. It occurs to me that perhaps it's all because she's a novelist.

At that moment, I suddenly remember that I didn't ask her for her address. I turn around to call out to her. But she's already disappeared out of view. Where could she have gone? I look down at the book in my hand. When I see the book, I get the feeling that I'll be able to write her a letter anytime, even if I don't ask her.

134. I mail the letter I wrote to Number 1, and call my friend.

As soon as he picks up, he asks me in a worried voice, "Are you feeling all right?"

"Yeah," I say.

"About the letters . . ." he begins.

"It doesn't matter anymore, whether they've come or not," I interrupt.

"How come?"

"I'm coming home today. I won't be waking you up with phone calls anymore, either."

"Is it because of the fire?"

"Wajo is a little sick."

"Where? Why? Is he hurt?"

"No, he isn't, but he needs some rest because he's got some problems."

"I guess Wajo is getting old, too."

"You've done so much for me."

"Don't mention it. Thanks to you, I got into the habit of getting up early."

"I guess that habit will go away soon."

"I was a bum when you left, and I'm still a bum."

My friend seems to be reflecting anew on the past three years. But he, too, must have changed in some way in those three years. Just as I have.

"Hurry up. I miss you. I just found an amazing girl, as it happens. Real deadly this time. It'd be a shame if only I got to see her," he says.

"Sure, show me when I get back," I say.

He's always been a little annoyed by the phone calls, but he must have been a little sad to think that one of his daily habits would come to an end. Our conversation lasted much longer than usual. It's always sad to say goodbye to a habit. Especially if it's contributed to the peace in your heart and in your daily life. Just as my journey has. Now I must get into a different kind of habit, and find myself in a different kind of life. For genuine peace and stability of mind.

I come out of the phone booth and hail a taxi. I've traveled far, and must travel just as far to reach home. I want to give Wajo a sense of stability on that long road home. The taxi comes to a stop. Wajo and I set out on the road, just the two of us without the woman. The time we spent with her was nothing compared to the three years of our journey, so why do I feel so empty inside? I must've grown used to traveling with her, for it feels a little strange to be left without her. Habits do have great power, indeed.

The taxi starts moving quietly with us inside. And so I say goodbye to the last city in which I stayed.

135. I didn't check with my friend, but probably, no one wrote me.

136. I reach home only when the day has grown dark.

It takes a long time, after the taxi leaves, for me to get up the courage to walk up to the door as if I'm snooping around someone else's house. The house feels a little unfamiliar, and I feel a little afraid. I feel as if I've entered a world I do not know, and as if something has expanded and then contracted.

The first thing I notice is the mailbox, hanging on the right side of the gate like a heart. I gently slip my hand in. I feel cold air instead of hot vibration. My friend hadn't been lying to me on the phone. There's nothing there. The empty mailbox is cold inside, as if its heart stopped long ago. Its mouth is rusty as if it's never been opened. The back of my hand gets stained with rust as I pull my hand out.

I leave the mailbox behind and push the gate open with my fingertips. The gate, unlocked, creaks open. I step in quietly like a thief. Then I turn around and take a look beyond the gate, which I've just stepped through. Three years ago, my journey began with me stepping through that gate, and now, it comes to an end with me stepping through it again. Why does it feel as if the boundaries of the beginning and the end are so far apart, when in fact, they're much too close together. The sense of distance probably comes from the human habit of separating and classifying and distinguishing, which sets the human heart at ease. I turn around, trying to cross the boundaries, and walk past the long yard toward the front door. I pull the door handle. The door, unlocked as expected, opens quietly with a rusty sound.

The house receives me.

137. I put Wajo down on the living room floor, and go from room to room looking for Mother, Father, Older Brother, and Jiyun. They must not be home yet. They were always busy, and always came home late. Soon enough, they will be shocked at my quiet return.

The house is much too quiet, with no one here. Houses are bound to be quiet with no one there, but it's unusually quiet in here. The only thing moving in this quiet, still house is the clock hanging in each room. The only sound I hear is the sound of the clocks. The second hands of the clocks do not coincide with one another. They're a little confusing because they all have different tones and vibrations. But the sound of the clocks, if nothing else, seems to make the unfamiliar silence step back. I end up thinking that it's quite loud, even.

At that moment, I hear a different sound. I move toward the sound as if drawn by it. I come to a stop in front of the bathroom. I gently push the door with my fingertips, and it opens wide.

Water is dripping from the bathtub faucet like teardrops. A drop falls every five seconds. The sound fills up the bathroom. Someone must not have turned it off completely after taking a bath. I put on the slippers and go inside, and try turning it tight. The faucet, however, is turned off as tightly as it can be, and the water continues to drip at regular intervals. The faucet, it seems, is broken, not left on. For how long has it been broken? How many drops of water must have fallen down into the dark ground below while I was gone? I calculate in my mind. A drop every five seconds means . . . 12 drops a minute . . . 120 drops every ten minutes . . . 720 drops an hour . . . 17,280 drops a day . . . 6,307,200 drops a year . . . 18,921,600 drops in three years.

Would I, too, have thought of home once in a while if I'd known that water was dripping from the faucet? Would I also have felt an urge to come home once in a while? Would I then have been able to return home earlier? I think about fixing the faucet, but decide to leave it as it is. Instead, I plug up the tub with a rubber stopper so that the water may not leak. Drop by drop, the water will make the tub undulate like a lake in no time. I toy around with the silly idea of collecting the drops of water for the next three years. I finish the calculation in my head, and I want to see with my own eyes how much 18,921,600 drops of water would be. I also want to touch the water to see how long three years are, and dip myself in the water.

I chuckle, thinking how silly I am, and turn away from the faucet. I can still hear very clearly the sound of water dripping behind me. It sounds like the sound of teardrops in a way, and the sound of blood, in a way. The sound grows louder and louder, like the sound of someone crying, and then spreads throughout the house like an epidemic. As if the only sounds made in the past three years were the sounds of water dripping and clocks ticking. It was a message for me, trying to tell me something, no, insisting something.

138. I have no family. No mother, no father, no brother, no Jiyun . . . Not one of them exists.

139. I'm still lying face down on the tile floor, unable to get up. The cold pieces of tile absorb the other pieces around them before my eyes, expanding their boundaries. The pieces of tile have turned into a gigantic screen which presents itself before my eyes. Images from that day are projected onto the screen, like an incredibly vivid dream. There's a sound of people talking loudly, and a strange smell, a message is conveyed, I am running somewhere, my heart beats, and then stops . . .

140. It was almost impossibly bright and sunny that day. People said that my grandfather was a blessed man. That he was blessed to have passed away on such a great day. The day my grandfather was being taken to the burial plot, my family had been in a rush since morning. My family must have had the same thought, for everyone got dressed without looking sad, and even had a good breakfast. I seem to remember that someone laughed, even. I was the one, actually, who was depressed to the point of death on that bright and sunny day.

An hour before we were to leave for the burial site, a registered letter, seemingly urgent, was delivered to me. I opened it in haste. It was a letter consisting of a very short sentence, and didn't take even five seconds to read. But in that short sentence that took five seconds to read were all of the 17,520 hours I had spent with my ex-girlfriend. Her letter stunned me. I was stunned that two years could be obliterated by that short sentence alone; that there was a sentence in the world that could more than obliterate two years; and more than anything, that she had created such a great, incredible sentence. It was a bizarre letter that kept you from saying anything at all, or imagining anything at all.

My family all got in the car to go to the burial site, regardless of my misfortune, even unaware, of what misfortune had befallen me. I crammed the letter into the pocket of my mourning clothes, and got in the car last. The day continued bright and sunny on our way to the burial site. The absurd weather threw me into fits of rage. I took the letter out again and read it. I could not tolerate this way of saying goodbye. I asked my father to stop the car, saying I had to go somewhere. My father asked me why, but I just let the tears fall without a word. My family looked solemn for a moment, probably thinking that I was crying because of my grandfather. My father, recalling that no one had cried that morning when we were about to bury my grandfather in the ground, stopped the car for me.

As soon as I got out of the car, I hailed a taxi and got in, tightly clutching the letter in my pocket. To me, breaking up with my girlfriend seemed something more awful and incomprehensible than burying my grandfather, who had gone forever to heaven. It wasn't as if my dead grandfather would come back to life if I arrived early at the burial site. But I could surely make my girlfriend come back to me. If I didn't do anything now, she would be gone forever, and if I didn't do anything, I'd have nothing but regret down the road.

I looked everywhere she was likely to be, beginning with her house. I ran and ran, to the point that I thought my heart would burst. It felt as if I had run halfway around the earth. But she was nowhere to be found. As if she'd never existed on the earth in the first place.

In the end, I didn't see her that day, and didn't see my grandfather take his last step, either.

141. And I didn't see my family.

142. That evening at dusk, I received a strange phone call on my way home.

It was my grandmother. She told me something strange in a feeble voice, not making much sense. It was so strange that I hung up in haste without even realizing it. Then I called her back in a little while. Again in a feeble voice, she told me the rest of the story. It was a strange story about how, on its way back from the burial site, the car carrying my family had crashed into a car driven by a drunk driver and turned over. I thought my grandmother had gone crazy at last. I thought she had gone crazy from the sorrow of losing her husband.

I ran to the hospital in a frenzy. My heart pounded as though I had run halfway around the earth. Strangely, I went into the mortuary in my mourning clothes. Strangely, my mother, father, and Jiyun were lying still in their mourning clothes. Strangely, my older brother, who was in his mourning clothes, had survived and was lying in the intensive care unit. Strangely, I did not shed a single tear. Like a tightly closed faucet.

That night, like a miracle, my brother returned to consciousness for a brief moment. He looked at me, with enough awareness to recognize me. I clutched his hand, as if to say I wouldn't let go. Then I began to wail as if to beg him. To remain by my side . . . to stay . . . to live. The tears flowed without ceasing. As though from a broken faucet. At that moment, my brother's lips twitched slightly. I put my face near his lips.

"Do . . . what . . . you . . . want . . . with . . . your . . . life . . ." he said.

After he said those words, the strength left his hand. He didn't reach out for my hand, and he didn't look at me, either. Then in a moment, he stopped breathing. His last breath could be felt at the tip of my nose. It was a strangely good smell, the kind I hadn't smelled anywhere before, and probably wouldn't smell anywhere in the future. Do what you want . . . he had woken up momentarily to say those words to me. I looked at his sleeping face. The look on his face seemed to say that he had grown weary of life. I think he put on that expression on purpose.

143. After that, I realized that everything in life happens in a day.

144. Wajo and I are here at the house, where there were sounds of only water dripping and clocks ticking. The sounds have grown richer because of Wajo and me. There's the sound of Wajo's shallow breathing, as well as of tossing and turning, and of my seizures. Many sounds accompany my seizures. My seizures have not been healed at all. The human body can make a great many sounds. That's because the body is an instrument, too. The closer it gets to death, the more dissonance the broken body creates. Still, I feel comforted to think I have Wajo by my side.

But even that comfort is not to be mine.

145. Wajo has died.

146. He died a day after we came home, as though he had just been waiting to come home. Wajo, who I once thought had killed me, has saved me in the end, and died. I think Wajo had been fighting it. Death, I mean. I think he'd been delaying the hour of his death because he wanted to die at home, where we once lived together, and not on a cold, strange street, or in a motel room where many people come and go.

My tears flow gently, quietly, and without a word, just like

Wajo. Wajo, lying at home, looks as peaceful as can be. Fortunately, his death comes without pain. Even that, I think, was out of his consideration for me. I'm at peace, too, because I'm able to send him off at home, not at a motel. At peace, I realize at last that he'd been at my side for me, not the other way around. I was happy, and never lonely, because of Wajo. For three years, I was always with someone.

I hold him tightly in my arms and whisper, "Wajo . . . Come to me as my puppy in your next life, too . . ."

147. I have no strength left in me, so my friend builds a coffin using a saw and a hammer, and digs up the ground on the sunniest spot in the front yard.

He stops digging for a moment and asks, "Should I dig deep?"

"No, make it shallow."

"I think we should make it deep."

"I think I'd feel like he was far away if it's deep."

"All right. Shallow, then . . ."

I place Wajo in the coffin. I give him another tight hug before I close the lid. My friend, who has been holding the lid, asks if he should close it now. I don't answer for a long time, and then finally nod my head. The coffin lid is blotting Wajo out little by little. I won't ever see that face again.

Wajo's coffin is lowered into the shallow ground. The weather is as sunny and bright as it was the day my grandfather was buried. Wajo is probably his guide dog again by now.

Covering the coffin with dirt and smoothing out the ground, my friend asks, "Still get those seizures?"

"Yeah."

"Come stay at my place if you're having a hard time."

"Your place is filthy."

"That's because I don't clean very often. It's clean when I do."

"I'll still be the same when I come back. I'll just stay here. Besides, Wajo's here."

"You need to see that girl I told you about. You never know when I'll get caught."

"I will soon."

"Cheer up. You look like you're about to be buried next to Wajo right now."

"I'll get better eventually."

"How about renting a small room and moving?"

"Moving? But I buried Wajo here."

"You can leave the house as it is. Then you can come see Wajo once in a while if you want."

Perhaps I'll do that, if my seizures don't stop.

"Do you want me to stay with you tonight?" he asks.

"Thanks," I accept.

148. The seizures subsided, thanks to my friend who stayed up talking to me all night. He even had breakfast with me. But he put his spoon down and ran out as soon as he got a phone call from his girlfriend, and the seizures returned. I can't swallow any more food. I clear the table and do the dishes. In his rush, my friend forgot his phone battery. The doorbell rings just then. He's so out of it. Without bothering to use the intercom, I push the button with a hand wearing a rubber glove. In the distance, I hear the sound of the gate latch coming undone.

I pour some detergent into the sink and wash the dishcloth. The friend I'm waiting for doesn't come; instead, I hear someone calling out to me. With my sudsy hands clasped together, I go to the front door.

"Young man, young man, are you home?" someone says.

I open the door. It's the woman from next door.

"I guess the supermarket lady was right when she said she saw you. How long has it been? When did you come home?" she asks.

"Three days ago . . ."

The woman, who has always been talkative, talks on and on as though to make up for the past three years. She sounds like someone who hasn't talked to anyone in all that time. All I can do is nod and say yes. The water on my rubber gloves has already dried off.

"Oh, I forgot. Let me go home for a second," she says.

She must have left a pot boiling on the stove or something. She probably wants to come back and talk on and on again. I feel a little tired, thinking I have to listen to her again. The woman, however, doesn't come back even after ten minutes, as if her house were a thousand miles away.

I go back into the kitchen and back to washing the dishcloth. The woman still isn't back. I twist the clean dishcloth tight to squeeze the water out. My mother always said that you had to squeeze out the water completely after washing dishcloths or rags. That if you didn't, something will happen to make you cry. Since I squeezed the water out completely, I don't think anything will happen to make me cry in the days ahead.

149. I'm about to go into my room when I hear the sound of the woman approaching, grunting as she comes. She comes in through the front door and puts down before me a package covered with invoices. It must originally have been a box holding a TV, for there's a picture of a TV on it.

"What's that?" I ask.

"Open it," she says.

I go up to the box and open it. When I see what's inside, I am stunned. I ask the woman because I can't seem to grasp what it is even after I take a look.

"What's all this?"

"Can't you tell? They're letters."

I check the letters one by one. They're all addressed to me. All the stamps have postmarks on them, and my name and address are clearly written out, indicating the recipient.

"How did you . . ." I begin.

"Mail kept coming for your family after you left on your trip. There was so much mail piled up later that some of it fell to the ground and got wet in the rain, so I made a request to the postman in charge. To deliver your family's mail to my house, because there was no one here," she explains.

I plop down on the floor. The woman looks a little surprised.

"What's wrong? Have I done something wrong?" she asks.

"No, I'm just feeling a little dizzy . . ." I say.

"Why do you get so many letters, anyway? I was quite surprised. At least two or three of them came for you every day—are they fan letters, or something?" she asks.

"No, they're just letters. Letters," I say.

Then I add, "Thank you . . ."

150. After the woman leaves, I take out the letters filling up the box one by one. They're all from numbers I know, addresses I know. No one gave me a false address. All the letters I sent arrived safely; it wasn't that the numbers didn't want to bother writing; it wasn't that they were illiterate; it wasn't that my letters got lost, or went unread; and it wasn't that the numbers died, or just disliked my letters. Everyone I wrote stayed alive and wrote me back. It wasn't true that no one had written me. I was never alone, not before my journey, not during my journey, and not after my journey.

In the end, my tears come spilling out. Even though I squeezed the water out completely from the dishcloth.

151. I read the letters all night, sitting on the sofa, without even eating. There are so many letters that I don't think I'll be able to read them all even when the night is over, or when the month is over. Still, I read each and every word. The letters make me laugh, make me cry, and make me sad, too. Some of the numbers even wrote me a second time because they didn't hear back from me. One of them told me that she and her boyfriend went to a motel I stayed at, and sent me a picture she took of the sentence I wrote on the sink there. There was also one who said he got into the habit of checking the sink when he went to a motel, and one who boasted, as though she had won the lottery, that she knew two motels that had sinks with sentences I'd written on them. One of the numbers complimented me on my neat handwriting, and the gum artist enclosed in his letter two tickets to his exhibition. Sadly, though, the date on the invitation had expired. 249, the high school girl, says that she was rewarded with a double eyelid surgery free of charge, a very successful one, too, for not squealing on her mother's extramarital affair, by the doctor her mother was having an affair with. She also said that after the surgery, she bought a book of poetry with her own money for the first time since she was born, and was now attending an acting school while preparing for the second time for college entrance, and asked me to cheer her on so that she'd be able to get into the drama and theater department. 109, the train vendor, tells me about the "little misunderstanding" that had taken control of his life. It was a little misunderstanding indeed. Now he's making good use of his major, with a fashion-related job. 367, who said that *gosiwons* were great buildings, is still living in the same building. He says he wants to move to one that's better equipped, but is hesitant because he hasn't heard back from me. He says he'll move when he gets a letter from me, and then tell me his new address. 412, who asked me to watch his stuff for him and went for a cup of coffee, explains why he never returned to the bus. While drinking his coffee, he got a phone call informing him of his friend's death and lost it in front of the vending machine. He, in fact, had been on his way that day to visit the friend he was supposed to introduce me to, because the friend was ill. The man who said he couldn't write unless he was in his room says that he has taken up writing novels again, and asks me if I could take a look at the novel he has finished writing recently. There's also a letter from 32, who traded shoelaces with me. He says that he recently bought a new pair of sneakers when he started a new business, but still wears my shoelaces with them. And finally, all the letters I wrote my family have arrived safely as well.

They're all in these letters. All the people I know are in these letters. I feel like I can live out the rest of my life just writing replies to these letters. What mystifies me is that my seizures have vanished completely after reading the letters. I don't think I'll ever have seizures again, as long as I keep receiving letters. Life is bearable when you have someone to write, and someone who writes you back. Even if it's just one person.

152. On my way to take out the trash, I notice two pieces of mail sticking out from the mailbox. It occurs to me in that moment that a mailbox is most like a mailbox when there's mail in it. I take out the mail. They're the first letters I take out from the mailbox. Now the mail is delivered properly to my house instead of the house next door.

I walk across the yard, looking at the letters. One is the letter I wrote to Number 1 at the last motel I stayed at. The letter I wrote to 1, the fellow traveler I met on the first day of my journey. The letter I wrote to Wajo, who had no language. It's arrived a bit late, so it must have gotten mixed up in the mail delivered next door. The woman from next door placed it in my mailbox on the sly.

I sit beside Wajo's grave and read the letter out loud for Wajo, who can't read. The letter is one of gratitude and apology. I think he understood me.

The second letter is from 751. I was going to write her first, but she beat me to it. How did she send the letter when I never told her my address? I open the blue envelope which looks as though she picked it out with care at a stationery shop. The first line holds the answer to my question. She begins the letter by saying that she took a peek at my address when she was mailing my letter for me. Her handwriting is so bad that it's nearly illegible. She has enclosed a picture. It's a picture of me pretending to be blind, wearing sunglasses, and of Wajo sitting faithfully next to me at the subway station. It's the first picture I took on my journey, and the first and last I took with Wajo. It has become a very valuable picture for me. Now I can see Wajo anytime.

At the close of her letter, she says that this letter she's sending me is the first one she's written on paper. She grumbles that she has wasted a lot of paper because she's used to writing on the computer. She says that she might have to reconsider if things go on the way they are, and goes off about how great e-mail is as she did once before. Reading that part, I felt my ears tingle as if she were chatting right next to me.

Finally, she adds a postscript at the end, saying that she's in the process of coming up with an idea for a novel with only one character in it. She also tells me that the novel is based on me.

After I finish reading the letter, there's a lot I want to say. I take the letter into my room and start writing her back immediately. I tell her about Wajo leaving my side; I thank her for sending me the picture; I tell her that tomorrow, I'm going to reopen my father's toy shop, that I'm reading *Toothpaste and Soap,* that I'll be living with my grandmother, that she should write letters with a pencil, and that water is dripping from the bathroom faucet. And that I have no intention of fixing it. And in addition, that this night on which I'm writing a letter to someone is as sublime as can be . . .

Jang Eun-jin was born in Gwangju, Korea, in 1976, and graduated from the Department of Geography at Cheonnam National University. She won the *Joongang Daily* New Writers Award for her debut, and has since published four novels and a collection of short stories.

Jung Yewon was born in Seoul, and moved to the U.S. at the age of 12. She received a BA in English from Brigham Young University, and an MA from the Graduate School of Interpretation and Translation at Hankuk University.

The Library of Korean Literature

The Library of Korean Literature, published by Dalkey Archive Press in collaboration with the Literature Translation Institute of Korea, presents modern classics of Korean literature in translation, featuring the best Korean authors from the late modern period through to the present day. The Library aims to introduce the intellectual and aesthetic diversity of contemporary Korean writing to English-language readers. The Library of Korean Literature is unprecedented in its scope, with Dalkey Archive Press publishing 25 Korean novels and short story collections in a single year.

The series is published in cooperation with the Literature Translation Institute of Korea, a center that promotes the cultural translation and worldwide dissemination of Korean language and culture.

SELECTED DALKEY ARCHIVE TITLES

MICHAL AJVAZ, *The Golden Age.*
　The Other City.
PIERRE ALBERT-BIROT, *Grabinoulor.*
YUZ ALESHKOVSKY, *Kangaroo.*
FELIPE ALFAU, *Chromos.*
　Locos.
IVAN ÂNGELO, *The Celebration.*
　The Tower of Glass.
ANTÓNIO LOBO ANTUNES, *Knowledge of Hell.*
　The Splendor of Portugal.
ALAIN ARIAS-MISSON, *Theatre of Incest.*
JOHN ASHBERY AND JAMES SCHUYLER, *A Nest of Ninnies.*
ROBERT ASHLEY, *Perfect Lives.*
GABRIELA AVIGUR-ROTEM, *Heatwave and Crazy Birds.*
DJUNA BARNES, *Ladies Almanack.*
　Ryder.
JOHN BARTH, *LETTERS.*
　Sabbatical.
DONALD BARTHELME, *The King.*
　Paradise.
SVETISLAV BASARA, *Chinese Letter.*
MIQUEL BAUÇÀ, *The Siege in the Room.*
RENÉ BELLETTO, *Dying.*
MAREK BIEŃCZYK, *Transparency.*
ANDREI BITOV, *Pushkin House.*
ANDREJ BLATNIK, *You Do Understand.*
LOUIS PAUL BOON, *Chapel Road.*
　My Little War.
　Summer in Termuren.
ROGER BOYLAN, *Killoyle.*
IGNÁCIO DE LOYOLA BRANDÃO,
　Anonymous Celebrity.
　Zero.
BONNIE BREMSER, *Troia: Mexican Memoirs.*
CHRISTINE BROOKE-ROSE, *Amalgamemnon.*
BRIGID BROPHY, *In Transit.*
GERALD L. BRUNS, *Modern Poetry and the Idea of Language.*
GABRIELLE BURTON, *Heartbreak Hotel.*
MICHEL BUTOR, *Degrees.*
　Mobile.
G. CABRERA INFANTE, *Infante's Inferno.*
　Three Trapped Tigers.
JULIETA CAMPOS,
　The Fear of Losing Eurydice.
ANNE CARSON, *Eros the Bittersweet.*
ORLY CASTEL-BLOOM, *Dolly City.*
LOUIS-FERDINAND CÉLINE, *Castle to Castle.*
　Conversations with Professor Y.
　London Bridge.
　Normance.
　North.
　Rigadoon.
MARIE CHAIX, *The Laurels of Lake Constance.*
HUGO CHARTERIS, *The Tide Is Right.*
ERIC CHEVILLARD, *Demolishing Nisard.*

MARC CHOLODENKO, *Mordechai Schamz.*
JOSHUA COHEN, *Witz.*
EMILY HOLMES COLEMAN, *The Shutter of Snow.*
ROBERT COOVER, *A Night at the Movies.*
STANLEY CRAWFORD, *Log of the S.S. The Mrs Unguentine.*
　Some Instructions to My Wife.
RENÉ CREVEL, *Putting My Foot in It.*
RALPH CUSACK, *Cadenza.*
NICHOLAS DELBANCO, *The Count of Concord.*
　Sherbrookes.
NIGEL DENNIS, *Cards of Identity.*
PETER DIMOCK, *A Short Rhetoric for Leaving the Family.*
ARIEL DORFMAN, *Konfidenz.*
COLEMAN DOWELL,
　Island People.
　Too Much Flesh and Jabez.
ARKADII DRAGOMOSHCHENKO, *Dust.*
RIKKI DUCORNET, *The Complete Butcher's Tales.*
　The Fountains of Neptune.
　The Jade Cabinet.
　Phosphor in Dreamland.
WILLIAM EASTLAKE, *The Bamboo Bed.*
　Castle Keep.
　Lyric of the Circle Heart.
JEAN ECHENOZ, *Chopin's Move.*
STANLEY ELKIN, *A Bad Man.*
　Criers and Kibitzers, Kibitzers and Criers.
　The Dick Gibson Show.
　The Franchiser.
　The Living End.
　Mrs. Ted Bliss.
FRANÇOIS EMMANUEL, *Invitation to a Voyage.*
SALVADOR ESPRIU, *Ariadne in the Grotesque Labyrinth.*
LESLIE A. FIEDLER, *Love and Death in the American Novel.*
JUAN FILLOY, *Op Oloop.*
ANDY FITCH, *Pop Poetics.*
GUSTAVE FLAUBERT, *Bouvard and Pécuchet.*
KASS FLEISHER, *Talking out of School.*
FORD MADOX FORD,
　The March of Literature.
JON FOSSE, *Aliss at the Fire.*
　Melancholy.
MAX FRISCH, *I'm Not Stiller.*
　Man in the Holocene.
CARLOS FUENTES, *Christopher Unborn.*
　Distant Relations.
　Terra Nostra.
　Where the Air Is Clear.
TAKEHIKO FUKUNAGA, *Flowers of Grass.*
WILLIAM GADDIS, *J R.*
　The Recognitions.

FOR A FULL LIST OF PUBLICATIONS, VISIT:
www.dalkeyarchive.com

SELECTED DALKEY ARCHIVE TITLES

JANICE GALLOWAY, *Foreign Parts*.
  The Trick Is to Keep Breathing.
WILLIAM H. GASS, *Cartesian Sonata
  and Other Novellas*.
  Finding a Form.
  A Temple of Texts.
  The Tunnel.
  Willie Masters' Lonesome Wife.
GÉRARD GAVARRY, *Hoppla! 1 2 3*.
ETIENNE GILSON,
  The Arts of the Beautiful.
  Forms and Substances in the Arts.
C. S. GISCOMBE, *Giscome Road*.
  Here.
DOUGLAS GLOVER, *Bad News of the Heart*.
WITOLD GOMBROWICZ,
  A Kind of Testament.
PAULO EMÍLIO SALES GOMES, *P's Three
  Women*.
GEORGI GOSPODINOV, *Natural Novel*.
JUAN GOYTISOLO, *Count Julian*.
  Juan the Landless.
  Makbara.
  Marks of Identity.
HENRY GREEN, *Back*.
  Blindness.
  Concluding.
  Doting.
  Nothing.
JACK GREEN, *Fire the Bastards!*
JIŘÍ GRUŠA, *The Questionnaire*.
MELA HARTWIG, *Am I a Redundant
  Human Being?*
JOHN HAWKES, *The Passion Artist*.
  Whistlejacket.
ELIZABETH HEIGHWAY, ED., *Contemporary
  Georgian Fiction*.
ALEKSANDAR HEMON, ED.,
  Best European Fiction.
AIDAN HIGGINS, *Balcony of Europe*.
  Blind Man's Bluff
  Bornholm Night-Ferry.
  Flotsam and Jetsam.
  Langrishe, Go Down.
  Scenes from a Receding Past.
KEIZO HINO, *Isle of Dreams*.
KAZUSHI HOSAKA, *Plainsong*.
ALDOUS HUXLEY, *Antic Hay*.
  Crome Yellow.
  Point Counter Point.
  Those Barren Leaves.
  Time Must Have a Stop.
NAOYUKI II, *The Shadow of a Blue Cat*.
GERT JONKE, *The Distant Sound*.
  Geometric Regional Novel.
  Homage to Czerny.
  The System of Vienna.
JACQUES JOUET, *Mountain R*.
  Savage.
  Upstaged.

MIEKO KANAI, *The Word Book*.
YORAM KANIUK, *Life on Sandpaper*.
HUGH KENNER, *Flaubert*.
  Joyce and Beckett: The Stoic Comedians.
  Joyce's Voices.
DANILO KIŠ, *The Attic*.
  Garden, Ashes.
  The Lute and the Scars
  Psalm 44.
  A Tomb for Boris Davidovich.
ANITA KONKKA, *A Fool's Paradise*.
GEORGE KONRÁD, *The City Builder*.
TADEUSZ KONWICKI, *A Minor Apocalypse*.
  The Polish Complex.
MENIS KOUMANDAREAS, *Koula*.
ELAINE KRAF, *The Princess of 72nd Street*.
JIM KRUSOE, *Iceland*.
AYŞE KULIN, *Farewell: A Mansion in
  Occupied Istanbul*.
EMILIO LASCANO TEGUI, *On Elegance
  While Sleeping*.
ERIC LAURRENT, *Do Not Touch*.
VIOLETTE LEDUC, *La Bâtarde*.
EDOUARD LEVÉ, *Autoportrait*.
  Suicide.
MARIO LEVI, *Istanbul Was a Fairy Tale*.
DEBORAH LEVY, *Billy and Girl*.
JOSÉ LEZAMA LIMA, *Paradiso*.
ROSA LIKSOM, *Dark Paradise*.
OSMAN LINS, *Avalovara*.
  The Queen of the Prisons of Greece.
ALF MAC LOCHLAINN,
  The Corpus in the Library.
  Out of Focus.
RON LOEWINSOHN, *Magnetic Field(s)*.
MINA LOY, *Stories and Essays of Mina Loy*.
D. KEITH MANO, *Take Five*.
MICHELINE AHARONIAN MARCOM,
  The Mirror in the Well.
BEN MARCUS,
  The Age of Wire and String.
WALLACE MARKFIELD,
  Teitlebaum's Window.
  To an Early Grave.
DAVID MARKSON, *Reader's Block*.
  Wittgenstein's Mistress.
CAROLE MASO, *AVA*.
LADISLAV MATEJKA AND KRYSTYNA
  POMORSKA, EDS.,
  *Readings in Russian Poetics:
    Formalist and Structuralist Views*.
HARRY MATHEWS, *Cigarettes*.
  The Conversions.
  *The Human Country: New and
    Collected Stories*.
  The Journalist.
  My Life in CIA.
  Singular Pleasures.
  *The Sinking of the Odradek
    Stadium*.
  Tlooth.

FOR A FULL LIST OF PUBLICATIONS, VISIT:
www.dalkeyarchive.com

JOSEPH MCELROY,
  Night Soul and Other Stories.
ABDELWAHAB MEDDEB, *Talismano.*
GERHARD MEIER, *Isle of the Dead.*
HERMAN MELVILLE, *The Confidence-Man.*
AMANDA MICHALOPOULOU, *I'd Like.*
STEVEN MILLHAUSER, *The Barnum Museum.*
  In the Penny Arcade.
RALPH J. MILLS, JR., *Essays on Poetry.*
MOMUS, *The Book of Jokes.*
CHRISTINE MONTALBETTI, *The Origin of Man.*
  Western.
OLIVE MOORE, *Spleen.*
NICHOLAS MOSLEY, *Accident.*
  Assassins.
  Catastrophe Practice.
  Experience and Religion.
  A Garden of Trees.
  Hopeful Monsters.
  Imago Bird.
  Impossible Object.
  Inventing God.
  Judith.
  Look at the Dark.
  Natalie Natalia.
  Serpent.
  Time at War.
WARREN MOTTE,
  *Fables of the Novel: French Fiction
    since 1990.*
  *Fiction Now: The French Novel in
    the 21st Century.*
  *Oulipo: A Primer of Potential
    Literature.*
GERALD MURNANE, *Barley Patch.*
  Inland.
YVES NAVARRE, *Our Share of Time.*
  Sweet Tooth.
DOROTHY NELSON, *In Night's City.*
  Tar and Feathers.
ESHKOL NEVO, *Homesick.*
WILFRIDO D. NOLLEDO, *But for the Lovers.*
FLANN O'BRIEN, *At Swim-Two-Birds.*
  The Best of Myles.
  The Dalkey Archive.
  The Hard Life.
  The Poor Mouth.
  The Third Policeman.
CLAUDE OLLIER, *The Mise-en-Scène.*
  Wert and the Life Without End.
GIOVANNI ORELLI, *Walaschek's Dream.*
PATRIK OUŘEDNÍK, *Europeana.*
  The Opportune Moment, 1855.
BORIS PAHOR, *Necropolis.*
FERNANDO DEL PASO, *News from the
  Empire.*
  Palinuro of Mexico.
ROBERT PINGET, *The Inquisitory.*
  Mahu or The Material.
  Trio.
MANUEL PUIG, *Betrayed by Rita Hayworth.*

The Buenos Aires Affair.
Heartbreak Tango.
RAYMOND QUENEAU, *The Last Days.*
  Odile.
  Pierrot Mon Ami.
  Saint Glinglin.
ANN QUIN, *Berg.*
  Passages.
  Three.
  Tripticks.
ISHMAEL REED, *The Free-Lance Pallbearers.*
  The Last Days of Louisiana Red.
  Ishmael Reed: The Plays.
  Juice!
  Reckless Eyeballing.
  The Terrible Threes.
  The Terrible Twos.
  Yellow Back Radio Broke-Down.
JASIA REICHARDT, *15 Journeys Warsaw
    to London.*
NOËLLE REVAZ, *With the Animals.*
JOÃO UBALDO RIBEIRO, *House of the
    Fortunate Buddhas.*
JEAN RICARDOU, *Place Names.*
RAINER MARIA RILKE, *The Notebooks of
    Malte Laurids Brigge.*
JULIÁN RÍOS, *The House of Ulysses.*
  Larva: A Midsummer Night's Babel.
  Poundemonium.
  Procession of Shadows.
AUGUSTO ROA BASTOS, *I the Supreme.*
DANIÈL ROBBERECHTS, *Arriving in Avignon.*
JEAN ROLIN, *The Explosion of the
    Radiator Hose.*
OLIVIER ROLIN, *Hotel Crystal.*
ALIX CLEO ROUBAUD, *Alix's Journal.*
JACQUES ROUBAUD, *The Form of a
    City Changes Faster, Alas, Than
    the Human Heart.*
  The Great Fire of London.
  Hortense in Exile.
  Hortense Is Abducted.
  The Loop.
  Mathematics:
  The Plurality of Worlds of Lewis.
  The Princess Hoppy.
  Some Thing Black.
RAYMOND ROUSSEL, *Impressions of Africa.*
VEDRANA RUDAN, *Night.*
STIG SÆTERBAKKEN, *Siamese.*
  Self Control.
LYDIE SALVAYRE, *The Company of Ghosts.*
  The Lecture.
  The Power of Flies.
LUIS RAFAEL SÁNCHEZ,
  Macho Camacho's Beat.
SEVERO SARDUY, *Cobra & Maitreya.*
NATHALIE SARRAUTE,
  Do You Hear Them?
  Martereau.
  The Planetarium.

ARNO SCHMIDT, *Collected Novellas.*
Collected Stories.
Nobodaddy's Children.
Two Novels.
ASAF SCHURR, *Motti.*
GAIL SCOTT, *My Paris.*
DAMION SEARLS, *What We Were Doing*
and Where We Were Going.
JUNE AKERS SEESE,
Is This What Other Women Feel Too?
What Waiting Really Means.
BERNARD SHARE, *Inish.*
Transit.
VIKTOR SHKLOVSKY, *Bowstring.*
Knight's Move.
A Sentimental Journey:
Memoirs 1917–1922.
Energy of Delusion: A Book on Plot.
Literature and Cinematography.
Theory of Prose.
Third Factory.
Zoo, or Letters Not about Love.
PIERRE SINIAC, *The Collaborators.*
KJERSTI A. SKOMSVOLD, *The Faster I Walk,*
the Smaller I Am.
JOSEF ŠKVORECKÝ, *The Engineer of*
Human Souls.
GILBERT SORRENTINO,
Aberration of Starlight.
Blue Pastoral.
Crystal Vision.
Imaginative Qualities of Actual
Things.
Mulligan Stew.
Pack of Lies.
Red the Fiend.
The Sky Changes.
Something Said.
Splendide-Hôtel.
Steelwork.
Under the Shadow.
W. M. SPACKMAN, *The Complete Fiction.*
ANDRZEJ STASIUK, *Dukla.*
Fado.
GERTRUDE STEIN, *The Making of Americans.*
A Novel of Thank You.
LARS SVENDSEN, *A Philosophy of Evil.*
PIOTR SZEWC, *Annihilation.*
GONÇALO M. TAVARES, *Jerusalem.*
Joseph Walser's Machine.
Learning to Pray in the Age of
Technique.
LUCIAN DAN TEODOROVICI,
Our Circus Presents . . .
NIKANOR TERATOLOGEN, *Assisted Living.*
STEFAN THEMERSON, *Hobson's Island.*
The Mystery of the Sardine.
Tom Harris.
TAEKO TOMIOKA, *Building Waves.*

JOHN TOOMEY, *Sleepwalker.*
JEAN-PHILIPPE TOUSSAINT, *The Bathroom.*
Camera.
Monsieur.
Reticence.
Running Away.
Self-Portrait Abroad.
Television.
The Truth about Marie.
DUMITRU TSEPENEAG, *Hotel Europa.*
The Necessary Marriage.
Pigeon Post.
Vain Art of the Fugue.
ESTHER TUSQUETS, *Stranded.*
DUBRAVKA UGRESIC, *Lend Me Your*
Character.
Thank You for Not Reading.
TOR ULVEN, *Replacement.*
MATI UNT, *Brecht at Night.*
Diary of a Blood Donor.
Things in the Night.
ÁLVARO URIBE AND OLIVIA SEARS, EDS.,
Best of Contemporary Mexican Fiction.
ELOY URROZ, *Friction.*
The Obstacles.
LUISA VALENZUELA, *Dark Desires and*
the Others.
He Who Searches.
PAUL VERHAEGHEN, *Omega Minor.*
AGLAJA VETERANYI, *Why the Child Is*
Cooking in the Polenta.
BORIS VIAN, *Heartsnatcher.*
LLORENÇ VILLALONGA, *The Dolls' Room.*
TOOMAS VINT, *An Unending Landscape.*
ORNELA VORPSI, *The Country Where No*
One Ever Dies.
AUSTRYN WAINHOUSE, *Hedyphagetica.*
CURTIS WHITE, *America's Magic Mountain.*
The Idea of Home.
Memories of My Father Watching TV.
Requiem.
DIANE WILLIAMS, *Excitability:*
Selected Stories.
Romancer Erector.
DOUGLAS WOOLF, *Wall to Wall.*
Ya! & John-Juan.
JAY WRIGHT, *Polynomials and Pollen.*
The Presentable Art of Reading
Absence.
PHILIP WYLIE, *Generation of Vipers.*
MARGUERITE YOUNG, *Angel in the Forest.*
Miss MacIntosh, My Darling.
REYOUNG, *Unbabbling.*
VLADO ŽABOT, *The Succubus.*
ZORAN ŽIVKOVIĆ, *Hidden Camera.*
LOUIS ZUKOFSKY, *Collected Fiction.*
VITOMIL ZUPAN, *Minuet for Guitar.*
SCOTT ZWIREN, *God Head.*